He was the kind of man who could make a woman go weak in the knees—about two seconds before she went soft in the head.

He wasn't pretty-boy handsome, but he *was* intensely male. His jaw was stubbled, there were dark shadows beneath his eyes and a silvery scar sliced across one cheekbone.

The stranger's head came up then, as if he'd suddenly registered her concentrated attention from across the room. His gaze in that first moment was frankly, sharply male, making her instantly aware of how male he was. And how female *she* was.

Roma's stomach lurched as his gaze locked on her again. Now she could see that his eyes were a pure, intense dark blue, wolf-cold and uncompromising. The jolting awareness escalated.

So *this* was Ben McCabe—her new bodyguard....

Dear Reader,

There's so much great reading in store for you this
month that it's hard to know where to begin, but I'll start
with bestselling author and reader favorite Fiona Brand.
She's back with another of her irresistible Alpha heroes
in *Marrying McCabe*. There's something about those
Aussie men that a reader just can't resist—and heroine
Roma Lombard is in the same boat when she meets
Ben McCabe. He's got trouble—and passion—written
all over him.

Our FIRSTBORN SONS continuity continues with
Born To Protect, by Virginia Kantra. Follow ex-Navy
SEAL Jack Dalton to Montana, where his princess
(and I mean that literally) awaits. A new book by
Ingrid Weaver is always a treat, so save some reading
time for *Fugitive Hearts*, a perfect mix of suspense
and romance. Round out the month with new novels by
Linda Castillo, who offers *A Hero To Hold* (and trust me,
you'll definitely want to hold this guy!); Barbara Ankrum,
who proves the truth of her title, *This Perfect Stranger*;
and Vickie Taylor, with *The Renegade Steals a Lady* (and
also, I promise, your heart).

And if that weren't enough excitement for one month, don't
forget to enter our Silhouette Makes You a Star contest.
Details are in every book.

Enjoy!

Leslie J. Wainger
Executive Senior Editor

FIONA BRAND
Marrying
McCabe

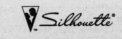

INTIMATE MOMENTS™

Published by Silhouette Books

America's Publisher of Contemporary Romance

To Leslie Wainger

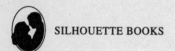

SILHOUETTE BOOKS

ISBN 0-373-27169-7

MARRYING McCABE

Visit Silhouette at www.eHarlequin.com

Printed in U.S.A.

Books by Fiona Brand

Silhouette Intimate Moments

Cullen's Bride #914
Heart of Midnight #977
Blade's Lady #1023
Marrying McCabe #1099

FIONA BRAND

has always wanted to write. After working eight years for the New Zealand Forest Service as a clerk, she decided she could spend at least that much time trying to get a romance novel published. Luckily, it only took five years, not eight. Fiona lives in a subtropical fishing and diving paradise called the Bay of Islands with her husband and two children.

SILHOUETTE MAKES YOU A STAR!
Feel like a star with Silhouette.
Look for the exciting details of our new contest
inside all of these fabulous Silhouette novels:

Romance

MAITLAND MATERNITY
#1540 A Very Special Delivery
Myrna Mackenzie

 DESTINY, TEXAS
#1541 This Kiss
Teresa Southwick

The Cinderella Conspiracy
#1542 Cinderella After Midnight
Lilian Darcy

#1543 Marrying for a Mom
DeAnna Talcott

THE WEDDING LEGACY
#1544 Wed by a Will
Cara Colter

#1545 Her Secret Longing
Gail Martin

Special Edition

Soldiers of Fortune
#1417 The Last Mercenary
Diana Palmer

THE CALAMITY JANES
#1418 To Catch a Thief
Sherryl Woods

#1419 When I Dream of You
Laurie Paige

#1420 Another Man's Children
Christine Flynn

#1421 Her Secret Affair
Arlene James

 THE BABY OF THE MONTH CLUB
#1422 An Abundance of Babies
Marie Ferrarella

Desire

MAN OF THE MONTH
#1387 The Millionaire Comes Home
Mary Lynn Baxter

#1388 Comanche Vow
Sheri WhiteFeather

20 AMBER COURT
#1389 When Jayne Met Erik
Elizabeth Bevarly

 THE FORTUNES of TEXAS
#1390 Fortune's Secret Daughter
Barbara McCauley

#1391 Sleeping with the Sultan
Alexandra Sellers

#1392 The Bridal Arrangement
Cindy Gerard

Intimate Moments

#1099 Marrying McCabe
Fiona Brand

FIRSTBORN SONS
#1100 Born To Protect
Virginia Kantra

#1101 Fugitive Hearts
Ingrid Weaver

#1102 A Hero To Hold
Linda Castillo

#1103 This Perfect Stranger
Barbara Ankrum

#1104 The Renegade Steals a Lady
Vickie Taylor

Chapter 1

The shot snapped through the humid Sydney night air, slicing through the cheerful hum of conversation as a steady stream of people exited the cinema complex. The flat one-two echo syncopated with the flash and burn of neon, a sharp counterpoint to the gentle nostalgia of rhythm and blues, the rich scent of coffee, the cloying vanilla of doughnuts and the edgier undernote of car exhaust and city grime.

Roma Lombard was jerked backward. The movement was violently at odds with the instant freeze-frame of humanity as the crowd, high on the latest romantic comedy, became eerily still, reacting as one creature with instincts that were ancient—primitive—at odds with the sleek, sophisticated cars lining the street, the expensive glitter of shop windows.

Her arms flailed as she fought to regain her balance. Her elbow glanced off the warm solidity of muscle; then a heavy shove sent her backward in an awkward sprawl, loose hair flinging in a dark veil across her face. The back of her head connected with concrete, detonating a burst of hot light behind her eyes.

For a dazed moment she lay stunned, held in thrall by the dazzling shift of colour, the shock of the fall; then something heavy slammed into her chest, punching all the breath from her lungs.

For long seconds she couldn't breathe, couldn't see, couldn't feel beyond the pain spiking her head, the stifling panic of being blinded by her own hair and the heavy weight pinning her—Lewis's weight, she realised.

He moaned. The sound was oddly soft, distressing, sending fear and adrenaline kicking through her veins. The sharp crack had been a rifle shot, and Lewis wasn't moving. Roma knew she hadn't been hit. Confusion and bruises aside, she'd simply been knocked off balance, but Lewis...Lewis was *hurt*.

A fierce sense of disbelief gripped her as she dragged her hair from her face, her mouth, logged the sting of grazes on her elbows, the blur of movement as the street cleared, followed by a spreading silence, as if the whole city was holding its breath.

Her isolation registered, and all the small hairs at her nape lifted on a cold ripple of awareness as she struggled to push against Lewis's weight. She didn't know how badly he was hurt, but suddenly even that consideration was secondary. They were stranded on the empty sidewalk, spot-lighted by the glare of cinema lights, an easy bull's-eye for even an amateur gunman. She had to get them both off the street.

She shoved at Lewis. The throb in her head kicked savagely, and she broke out in a clammy sweat. The heat she'd loved just seconds ago now closed around her like a vice. Time crawled—oddly suspended—she could feel the weight of every second as if it were her last, hammering in time with the thud of her heart, equated each beat with another shot from the rifle.

She wrenched upward, stomach muscles straining as she braced herself for more leverage, thankful her arms and shoulders were strong, her body tight and toned from regular exercise and the occasional work-out with weights. Lewis wasn't a heavy man, but he was tall—a gangly computer nerd rather than a muscled athlete. It didn't matter; Roma wasn't much over five foot five, so shifting him was like pushing against a mountain.

Gritting her teeth, she shoved again, twisting as she did so. Fear gave her the extra strength she needed to move Lewis's bulk enough that she could shimmy free and roll him onto his back.

He moaned again and stirred. His eyes flickered, half opened. "Roma?"

His voice was croaky, a thread of his normal light baritone. His eyes were unfocused, his breathing fast, face pale and shiny with sweat as he clutched at his shoulder and winced. Blood leaked from between his fingers, the spreading patch dark against his ridiculously cheerful Hawaiian shirt.

"Don't move." Roma wrenched Lewis's hand away and forgot about diving for cover, forgot there was a gunman. Her mind spun into overdrive as she shoved the heel of her palm against his shoulder, planted her other hand on top of the first, and leaned into the wound, using her weight to apply pressure. She'd done first aid courses—she knew the theory— but she'd never seen a gunshot wound before, and the violent reality of it was paralysing. She had to force her sluggish brain to think past the frightening blankness, to *remember*.

She began talking, her voice hollow, jerky, rising over Lewis's high-pitched moan as he tried to curl into a foetal ball, almost dislodging her hold as she explained what she was doing, that he had to be still, that she would get help.

Help.

Her head jerked up, gaze swinging wildly as she searched for assistance. She saw with a renewed sense of shock that she and Lewis were alone except for a couple crouched behind a nearby car. There were people huddled in the cinema complex; she could see faces peering out from behind movie posters. A man made eye contact with her and pointed at his cell phone as he talked rapidly into it.

Roma felt like closing her eyes against a raw

punch of disbelief. She was shaking with reaction and the aftershock of adrenaline, her arms and shoulders aching from the strain of her position, yet just minutes ago she'd been relaxed and happy, enjoying the upbeat atmosphere of the movie crowd, the balmy evening and Lewis's terrible jokes. She could still hear music, smell coffee and doughnuts. The city, the street, the night, were the same, yet in a split second everything else had changed. The protection of the crowd had melted away, leaving her kneeling, solitary and exposed, over Lewis.

Blood continued to well. In desperation, Roma wrenched off her shirt—not caring that she had only a bra on underneath—wadded the soft, white cotton into a pressure pad and jammed it over the wound, fisting it down tight.

The ambient air temperature was warm, she should have been fanning herself against the heat, but she didn't feel warm now. A slight breeze flipped hair across her face, slid over her almost-naked back, roughening her damp skin with the chill of invisible fingers. She noted that Lewis was no longer conscious, and fear formed an icy knot inside her.

Roma knew guns, knew how to handle them, break them down, clean and reassemble them. She knew how it felt to fire a gun, to ache in her arms and shoulders and wrists from spending long hours at shooting ranges. She knew more about guns than she had ever wanted to know, but she'd shied away from learning anything more than she had to about the damage they could do. The wound in Lewis's shoulder didn't look big, but that was no cause for celebration. Small-calibre rounds didn't make huge entry wounds, but they had a tendency to travel in the body, ricocheting off bone and causing immense soft tissue damage.

Her heart squeezed tight in her chest as she crouched over Lewis with all the fierceness of a lioness protecting her only cub. "Don't die," she commanded, her voice still husky, hollow.

His eyelids flickered, and she decided he'd heard her. He wouldn't die. She wouldn't allow it.

Lewis was her friend.

She could count the friends she had on one hand, and she cherished each and every one of them; they were as precious as family to her. She wasn't going to lose Lewis.

Briefly she closed her eyes against the hot sting of tears and sent up a prayer. He needed an ambulance—fast.

The distant wail of a siren jerked her head up. She craned around, dark gaze homing in on the direction of the siren, as if she could make help come faster with the sheer force of her will.

The street was completely empty of movement now, and unnaturally hushed. Traffic must have been cordoned off. Across the road, darkened apartments loomed over the bright facade of shop-fronts. Roma had barely, if ever, noticed those apartments, but in the aftermath of the shooting, they took on a faceless, menacing aspect. She'd consciously blocked the thought that the shot could have originated from any one of those blank windows. She'd been running on adrenaline, reacting rather than thinking, but now cold logic and a growing awareness of being watched, began to register.

She froze, head still craned at a painful angle, gaze still fixed in the direction of the siren. She'd felt that same creeping sensation before, the tension in the pit of her stomach, the abrupt sharpening of her senses, but she'd always dismissed it as paranoia.

The warm breeze swirled, turned chill against the taut curve of her throat, the naked arch of her back, so that she tensed against the convulsive need to shiver. The skin along her spine tightened with an almost painful sensitivity, twitched, as if a gun was now trained on the centre of her back, the gunman's finger stroking the trigger.

In that moment she felt her semi-nakedness, the sheer vulnerability of pale, exposed skin, the softness and fragility of flesh and bone.

A shudder rocked her and she had to fight the wild urge to fling herself flat on the pavement, belly-crawl behind a car and hide.

She hated the shattering sense of vulnerability, the cowardly impulse to save herself and leave Lewis bleeding on the sidewalk. She was a Lombard—for her, the threat of violence was no novelty—but she had never before felt directly threatened, never before felt so utterly powerless.

Images and impressions tumbled through her mind as the nightmare visions of a past that had haunted

her since she was fifteen flooded back, swamping
her.

Nine years ago Roma's eldest brother, Jake, and
his fiancée had been kidnapped and shot by a terrorist
group headed by a man named Egan Harper.

The shock of their deaths had hit her hard. She
hadn't been able to turn off her imagination or erase
the brutal details from her mind. She'd swung wildly
between impotent rage and an icy fear of the same
thing happening again to another member of her family.

She'd had counselling. It had helped, but no one
had been able to give her back the older brother she
loved, or the fragile illusion of safety. Harper had
shattered a basic innocence in them all that day.

In the years that followed, her family's vulnerability had been reinforced when Harper had continued to stalk them and had attempted to kill another
of her brothers, Gray, and the woman he'd married,
Sam. They had all breathed a collective sigh of relief
when Harper had been the one to die in that last
encounter.

Through it all, Roma had worked to achieve a
level of happiness and peace, unwilling to let Harper
take anything more from her than he already had.
She'd done a number of things to take control of her
life, including keeping fit, and taking martial arts and
gun classes, but the fact remained that safety *was*
only an illusion. Harper was dead, but he wasn't
alone out there.

Roma didn't see herself as paranoid. She was a

realist. The entire Lombard family was a target, not only because of their wealth and high media profile, but because a branch of the family business was tied up with the development of hi-tech arms and communication equipment for the military.

For them, it wasn't a matter of *if* trouble would strike, it was a matter of *when*.

Lewis stirred, his eyes flickering. Roma stared numbly at the grey pallor of his face, and rage built steadily inside her at what had been done to Lewis— bright, inoffensive, fun-loving Lewis, who wouldn't hurt a fly. Roma had the odd, fragmented thought that if she'd stayed at home, read a book or watched TV, instead of going out looking for bright lights and fun, tired of her own company, Lewis wouldn't be bleeding on the sidewalk now. No one would have gotten hurt.

The wail of the siren grew louder, then stopped, the abrupt silence punctuated by the shallow rasp of Lewis's breathing, the rapid thud of her heart shoving blood through her veins in short, shuddering bursts. For an oddly distorted period of time Roma was unable to breathe, as if a giant fist had closed around her lungs, squeezing them tight, shutting them down, so that her vision narrowed and dimmed, and sensation faded, as if she were no longer completely connected with her physical body.

So this was what it was like to go into shock.

She could have done with never finding out.

Chapter 2

Two days later.

Ben McCabe strode across the car park of Auckland's international airport. A gust of warm wind broadsided him as he stepped up on the kerb, forcing his already gritty eyes to narrow against the sting of dust whirling off the pavement. The acres of glass fronting the main terminal tossed his reflection back at him: crumpled T-shirt, jeans that were ripped at one knee, stubbled jaw and tired eyes.

There was a stain on his shoulder.

A disgusted groan scraped from Ben's throat as he passed through the doors and headed for the Arrivals lounge. The stain was small—little more than a narrow streak—but, on a white T-shirt, orange was definitely orange.

So much for looking like a hotshot security consultant, but he'd been too tired, in too much of a hurry—and too ticked off with the way Gray was calling in this favour with close to zero notice—to care what he'd looked like. He'd been pulled in from a camping trip with his daughter, and after driving half the night, he'd simply dropped Bunny at his mother's place, gone home, showered and crashed. When the alarm had rung, he'd gotten dressed in the dark. He'd hardly noticed what he'd shoved his arms and legs into.

Gray was one of the best friends he'd ever had, but in Ben's opinion, spending the next week playing bodyguard to his kid sister while she sashayed around all of Auckland's best society parties was more in the line of a pain in the ass than actual work.

By anyone's standards, Roma Lombard was rich and spoiled. She was the pampered only daughter of the wealthy Lombard hotelier family. Baby Roma hadn't been born with a silver spoon in her mouth; it had been diamond-encrusted platinum.

Ben wasn't impressed. He'd seen rich and spoiled, and he didn't like it. He should know. Once he'd been dumb enough to marry it, and his ex-wife, Nicola, had given him a crash course in hell he was in no mood to repeat.

A flash of dark humour momentarily lightened his mood. Not that he would be marrying Roma Lombard, just riding herd on her for the next couple of weeks. But in some ways personal bodyguarding was more intimate than being married. There was no walking out, no slamming doors—they would be stuck together, for better or worse, until he delivered her back to her doting big brother.

The information board confirmed that the red-eye flight from Sydney to Auckland had landed just minutes ago, along with a number of other flights. Ben scanned the steady stream of passengers pushing luggage trolleys. It was summer—school holidays—and the place was crazy with people flying in for a slice of Pacific paradise.

Ben couldn't get excited, not when he'd had to cancel his camping trip with his daughter and it looked as though he would be spending the next week with a spoiled brat.

His stomach rumbled, reminding him that dinner last night had been sketchy and he hadn't had time for breakfast. On top of everything else that was about to go wrong with today, he was hungry. Cursing beneath his breath, he began to pace.

Roma strolled with her brother, Gray, toward the luggage carousel, her mood going from bad to worse. She had a headache. She never had headaches. "I don't need twenty-four-hour protection," she said flatly. "I can't help Evan fund-raise with a bodyguard vetoing me at every turn."

"You're getting protection. It'll be discreet."

Discreet? Roma reined in her disbelief. After the scare just two days ago, her family had rallied around her like a bunch of hens around their only chick. As much as she loved them all, she'd had enough of all the concentrated attention and concern.

She knew she had to accept a certain level of security, but she hadn't bargained on a bodyguard. Unfortunately, her only alternative was to catch the next flight home, and there were two very good reasons why she wasn't going to do that. The first one was walking beside her. Any more of Gray's security precautions and she would go crazy. The second reason was that she'd given Evan diVaggio her promise to help months ago, and she wasn't backing out on him at the last minute.

Normally she didn't go near high-profile social events, because she hated the media attention, but Evan's crusade to fund a children's cancer ward was a special case. He was a long-time friend of the family, and she'd shared in his grief when his small nephew had died of an inoperable brain tumour. "Evan's not going to be happy."

Massive understatement.

Evan was artistic and temperamental; a successful fashion designer with his own exclusive house. He was a lot of fun—when he got his own way.

"The hell with Evan. Your safety's more important than his damn fashion show."

Gray gripped her elbow, guiding her through the thickening knots of people waiting to collect their bags. Roma did a slow, silent count to three, then disengaged Gray's hold with a practised twist of her arm. Her brothers had always treated her like a piece of delicate bone china, despite the fact that she'd been a tomboy ever since she was old enough to lace up a pair of sneakers and tag along after them. She'd never quite figured out their logic. They remembered she was female—usually at inconvenient times—but they seemed to forget that she had camped out with them, that she could outshoot the lot of them at pool, and that she had the meanest pitching arm in Lombard history. "*My* safety hasn't been directly threatened. And I gave Evan my promise months ago. I'm not letting some suit prevent me from meeting my commitments."

The set of Gray's jaw didn't alter. He'd been as upset as anyone about the loss of Evan's nephew, but she knew that, for Gray, his own family's safety was paramount. "We've already had this argument, honey. You're getting protection." His mouth quirked, the first sign of humour she'd seen in him for days. "I promise I haven't got you a G-man this time. Come on, let's find your bag. I don't want to miss my flight out."

Roma's eyes narrowed, her suspicions aroused by his comment. "Is he old?"

"Does it matter?"

"How old?"

"Old enough."

Roma drew a measured breath. The last bodyguard

she'd had had been forty going on eighty. He'd been so dour and humourless that, by the time his employment had come to an end, she'd decided the only person who had ever been in any danger had been him—from her.

If she had to practically live with someone, she wanted to have some control over who that person was. She knew, though, that Gray hadn't had time to let her pick and choose. When she'd refused to back out of the trip, he'd had to make arrangements in a hurry.

Gray's mouth kicked up at one corner. "Don't try it with this guy."

"Try what?" she muttered, knowing exactly what he meant. She'd been an unruly teenager and hell-on-wheels to watch—a reaction against the years her family had endured tight security. At times the pressure had been intolerable, and she'd lashed out against it in ways her family hadn't always appreciated. Despite the fact that she hadn't pulled a practical joke in years, that reputation for trouble had stuck.

"Don't try whatever plan is hatching in that serpentine mind of yours."

"I'm twenty-four, hardly a baby. And this is New Zealand, not some back alley in Beirut."

"You're a Lombard. For some people, that's enough." He gave her an irritated glance. "And what would you know about back alleys in Beirut?"

Roma's mouth curled lazily, delight filling her that

she'd actually put a nick in Gray's rock-solid control. She adored Gray, but sometimes he was too serious, too controlling. To Roma's way of thinking, her teasing was necessary; he needed someone to poke fun at him and temper all that omnipotent efficiency. Of course, he now had his wife, Sam, to fulfil that role. Since Gray had married and become a father, he had loosened up considerably. "Wouldn't you like to know?" she murmured.

Gray gave her an exasperated look that was all big brother. "Hell," he muttered. "That's precisely why you need a minder."

A familiar case appeared on the conveyor belt. Roma cut in front of Gray and snagged it before he could, blandly ignoring his irritation. He liked to be in charge, but she didn't exactly like being pushed aside, either. The result was occasionally an undignified tussle, but not without humour. It was a family thing.

Gray's mouth twitched. To pay her back, he gripped her elbow again as he urged her toward customs.

"I'm not an old lady," she grumbled.

"No," he agreed. "You're a smartass."

Minutes later, they approached the Arrivals lounge, and, humour and squabbling aside, Roma was glad for Gray's solid presence beside her, even if he'd sneakily taken charge of the trolley while she'd dug in her holdall for her passport.

It was busy in the terminal, filled with noise and

people, a baby crying, laughter. The acoustics amplified the sounds so that they built like a slow breaking wave. Tension gripped her as they took the final
turn into the large open area. She put the tension
down to a temporary paranoia that had developed
since Lewis's shooting—a knee-jerk reaction that
sneaked up on her every time she was in a public
place, which lately, between hospital visits and airport terminals, seemed to be most of the time.

She pulled in a deep breath, then another, willing
the ridiculous, *wimpy* feeling of exposure to disap-
pear, but her heart was still pounding as she searched
the busy lounge, trying to pick the bodyguard out of
the shifting mass of people. With the neat, dark suits
they invariably wore, the military-short haircuts,
cold, watchful eyes, and the discreet bulge of shoul-
der-holstered weapons, they might as well have been
in uniform.

No one fitted the description. Roma's knees actually went wobbly with relief. The magnitude of her
relief was in itself alarming. Over the years she'd
become aware that, for her, the severely suited bodyguards had become the symbol of her family's vulnerability, but she'd never reacted so violently to the
thought of having an armed escort before.

But then, you've never been shot at before.

Instantly she rejected the thought. The shooting
appeared to be a random one, the fact that Lewis had
been shot while he was with her pure coincidence. If
she'd been the target, the shooter had had plenty of

time to take aim and fire while she'd knelt over
Lewis waiting for the ambulance, but there hadn't
been a second shot. She'd been surrounded by armed
policemen and helped into the cover of a service lane
where an ambulance was parked. A shirt had been
magically produced and draped around her, envel-
oping her from neck to knee. Minutes later Lewis
had been loaded into the back of the ambulance on
a stretcher, and they had both been taken to the nearest hospital.

The police hadn't found any trace of the gunman,
or any reason for Lewis to be shot. The investigation
was still ongoing, but with no suspect, motive, or
weapon, there wasn't much hope that the perpetrator
would ever be caught, let alone his reason for shooting into a crowd ever discovered.

Roma's gaze settled on a big, rough-looking guy
who somehow managed to dominate the swirling sea
of people. Maybe because he was tall, six-foot-two
at least, and dark, with the kind of big, sleek build
that would always catch the feminine eye. He looked
like a man who would be at home in any era, just as
capable of defending his loved ones with a club or a
sword as with his bare fists.

In tight, faded jeans and a T-shirt that looked as
if it had survived a refugee parcel, no way did this
guy look like a bodyguard.

A wave of longing swept her, not for the man specifically, but for what he represented—an ordinary
life with ordinary goals such as family and children,

and deciding whether to have chicken or steak for dinner, of being able to have an ordinary nine-to-five job, live in a house without sophisticated security on every window and door, and go where she wanted, when she felt like it. Of being able to love those closest to her without fear they would be hurt or taken from her.

Unexpected tears burned her eyes. She blinked, pushing back the attack of the blues with a wave of grumpiness. So, okay, she was a mess—her *life* was a mess. Her head felt odd and floaty, because she had barely slept since the shooting. The headache that had no right to exist was getting worse. She was hungry. If anyone walked past her with food, she would probably attack them. And her brother was siccing a bodyguard on her.

Someone was going to pay for this.

"I don't want whatever suit you've picked out for me," she stated as Gray continued to forge a path across the lounge in the general direction of the tall, rough guy. "I want *him*."

Gray spared her a glance. His black gaze gleamed with amusement. "Want me to get him for you?"

Roma went still inside. That was not the answer she was expecting. Neither of her brothers was in the habit of "getting" men for her; they were more inclined to get rid of them. If they had their way, she would die a virgin. They were what she euphemistically termed overprotective.

She could count the boyfriends she'd had on two

hands, the ones who'd been brave enough to come home with her on one. If they weren't intimidated by her family's sheer wealth or the stringent security, her brothers usually managed to scare them off. There was nothing sophisticated about Gray and Blade's methods. Cold eye contact was always good for starters. A few pointed questions usually followed, and when neither of those strategies worked, her brothers resorted to blunt warnings that bordered on rudeness. Occasionally, if they happened to be out by the pool, there was a show of raw muscle—caveman tactics all the way.

Roma watched with growing suspicion as the tall stranger turned with an abrupt impatience that denoted someone who didn't want to be where he was and hated being kept waiting, and she saw his face clearly for the first time. Her stomach sank. Suddenly the stranger didn't look reassuring at all. He looked familiar.

He was tanned and muscular, black-haired, olive-skinned, all clean angles and blades, with a square jaw and deep-set eyes beneath straight brows. Not pretty-boy handsome, but with the kind of strong good looks that, coupled with his size and build, would make most women go weak at the knees about two seconds before they went soft in the head.

His jaw was darkly stubbled, as if he hadn't been near a razor for a couple of days, and there were dark shadows beneath his eyes as if he, too, hadn't had a lot of sleep lately. But the one detail that fixed

her attention was the scar that sliced across one
cheekbone. Whoever had sewn the wound closed
hadn't made a good job of it, and the scar tissue
skimming his tanned skin made him look more than
just casually dangerous. She'd seen that scar before
in photos, and woven more than a few fantasies about
that hard masculine face.

Ben McCabe. One of Gray and Blade's Special
Air Service cronies—possibly the only SAS agent
she hadn't yet met in the flesh.

His head came up as if he'd suddenly registered
her concentrated attention. His eyes were dark, slitted
with irritation, and something more. His gaze in that
first moment was frankly, sharply male. It was the
lightning perusal of a man who knew women intimately, not lingering so that she became uncomfortable, but making her instantly aware of how male he
was. And how female *she* was.

The abrupt awareness of her own sex startled
Roma. Her family's wealth and status usually provided a shield against this kind of overt attention,
and she seldom went out on dates. She was completely unprepared for the flood of heat that swept
her. The barrage of sensation was as overwhelming
as it was intrusive, and she fought back the only way
she knew how, by desperately trying to blank out all
emotion.

A group of teenagers in sports uniforms cut across
their path, momentarily blocking the man from view.

Roma's stomach lurched when the stranger's gaze

locked on her again. Now that she was closer, she could see that his eyes were a pure, intense dark blue, wolf-cold and uncompromising. The jolting awareness escalated, and with it came a solid dose of irritation.

"I've changed my mind," she muttered to Gray. "I don't want him. You win, I'll take the suit."

"Honey," Gray said, with a dry humour that made her want to strangle him, "McCabe *is* the suit."

Chapter 3

Ben fought back disbelief as he watched Gray approach, his hunger and frustration forgotten. The woman with Gray was his sister, but Roma Lombard wasn't what he'd expected.

He'd heard a lot about her—had even seen photographs of her. God only knew, her face was hard to miss when it was splashed across one of those glossy magazines his ex-wife used to read. But the glossy pictures he'd barely glanced at had nothing to do with the woman walking toward him now.

She wasn't tall enough to be a model; next to her brother, she was decidedly petite, even dainty. She wasn't wearing make-up or nail polish that he could see, no designer sunglasses or expensive designer clothes. Ben decided she didn't need any of those things. In a soft black shirt, faded jeans and black boots, she was pure fantasy material. Her silky dark hair hung in a straight, careless fall around her shoulders; her features were neat and even, her mouth soft. The only part of her that fulfilled anything like the image Ben had formed were the exotic eyes that continued to stare dazedly back at him. They were midnight-dark, shadowed by lashes, as distant and aloof as a cat's, and just as layered with mystery and secrets.

The blankness of her expression, the aura of sphinxlike remoteness, only served to intensify the mystery of her eyes, and Ben's jaw tightened against his response to that unconscious challenge. He was growing hard, his loins warming with a slow, heavy ache.

He suppressed a whole string of curses as he accepted Gray's handshake. Gray was a friend, more than a friend. And the woman Ben had been checking out was Gray's sister.

Out of bounds, way out of bounds. Even if she hadn't been his client.

Gray made the introductions. Grimly, Ben noted the brevity and firmness of Roma's handshake, as if she didn't want to touch him but wasn't about to flinch from it, the cool, minimal eye contact she allowed. Most people gave something of themselves away with their initial body language; Roma Lombard was notable by her very stillness.

Her controlled reserve only intrigued him more.

Ben was good at reading people—better than good—but Roma Lombard was an enigma. He considered the fact that the unexpected sexual attraction was messing up his perception, then discounted it. He was aroused, but he'd long ago learned to separate his intellect from his physical needs.

Her gaze connected with his, held just a little too long before she looked away again, a faint blush warming her cheekbones.

Damn, Ben thought mildly as Gray caught him up to date with news about mutual friends and Gray's brother, Blade, who'd just become a father. Either Roma disliked him intensely or she was as attracted as he was. Ben was betting on the second possibility.

He needed to hit something, preferably his head, against a wall, a block of stone, something that would hurt. Anything to take his mind off the fact that he was too interested in Ms. Lombard, and that most of his interest centred around backing her up against the nearest wall and seeing if she tasted as good as she looked.

Not that he would have to go looking for bruises. If Gray or Blade ever found out he'd fallen in instant lust with their sister, all the years of shared cama-raderie in the SAS wouldn't count for a thing.

His lashes drooped as he talked with Gray, shield-ing his intense interest in the woman he'd been hired to protect.

He could see why photographers went wild over her, why men dropped like flies. She wasn't flashy or charismatic; on the contrary, she was curiously understated, as if she kept even her own femininity under wraps.

Sweet hell, who was he trying to kid? She probably had that air of mystery perfected. Any man who ever looked at the lady would want her. No wonder Gray was tearing his hair out trying to keep her protected. Ben had been taken in by the aloof act, but he had to remember that she'd checked him out just as thoroughly as he'd done her.

She glanced at him again, and he discovered her eyes weren't black, as he'd first thought; they were a rich, velvety chocolate, bare shades lighter than the dark sable of her hair.

Ben almost groaned out loud. He *loved* chocolate. And he would have his work cut out swatting men off left, right and centre—and that would be when she wasn't sneaking them in the back door.

Some of the stories Gray and Blade used to tell about their cute little sister began to register. Roma was athletic and loved to run, and she hadn't confined her running to the sports field. She had run away as a teenager. She had also run rings around her bodyguards, destroying more than one reputation. Apparently she'd driven any number of security personnel crazy—one by keeping him out so late at nightclubs he'd barely been able to function during the day. Another had quit after a solid week of shopping. It had sounded funny at the time. Sitting in the jungle on extended patrol, soaking wet, eating reconstituted food, and wondering if someone was drawing a bead on his spine, Ben had grabbed at the humour and laughed at the antics of Baby Roma just as hard as Gray and Blade and the rest of the guys.

They'd even made up newspaper headlines: Bodyguard Found Dead In Mall: Autopsy Reveals Death By Shopping.

Ben wasn't laughing now. Roma Lombard might look like every man's fantasy, but she was trouble in capital letters.

His eyes narrowed. He'd be damned if he would let her run all over him.

At Gray's suggestion, they moved to a quieter part of the lounge. Ben accepted the envelope Gray extracted from his briefcase and automatically began examining the contents, but he was still having difficulty concentrating. His mind was firmly fixed on the one complication he could not afford—a sexual attraction to his client.

If he didn't owe Gray any number of favours, he would have dumped Ms. Lombard's sweet little ass on someone else's lap.

Chapter 4

Roma could still feel the heat of McCabe's touch. His palm had been warm, calloused, and so rough it had sent a hot shock of sensation up her arm.

Wearily, she assessed the situation. McCabe was her bodyguard, and she couldn't do a thing about it.

He was mouth-wateringly gorgeous, even better than his photos, and she wanted him.

Yep, just as she thought, her life had just officially gone to hell.

She'd heard McCabe's name mentioned often, although the actual personal information she knew about him was small. She knew he was a good friend of both Gray and Blade, and had been in the SAS with her brothers. He'd been married and was recently divorced, and he was now a single dad with custody of his child.

His blue gaze connected with hers again, and she decided she had one other piece of information. He didn't like her.

Good, she thought tartly, squashing her bewilderment and a ridiculous pang of hurt. She didn't want to be on intimate terms with McCabe. He was exactly the kind of male she didn't need in her life: dominant, overconfident, a real lady-killer.

Roma frowned when she identified a thread of excitement still twining through the long list of negatives she was building against McCabe, but she didn't question why she had to build a case against being attracted to him. He'd looked at her and she'd been turned on. The sudden attack of lust alarmed her, because she'd never lost control like that before.

His deep voice mingled with Gray's as he methodically flipped through printed material and a sheaf of enlarged black-and-white photos. The edgy, simmering impatience had disappeared and he now radiated the cool competency of a man who was used to danger and knew just what to do with it.

Faded jeans and T-shirt aside, McCabe looked like exactly what she knew him to be: a highly trained professional, an ex-SAS assault and anti-terrorist specialist who, from the conversation, was now in business as a security consultant.

He began firing questions at Gray. Finally he looked up from the material in his hands. "Either it was a random shooting or the shot was wide. Did you pinpoint a trajectory?"

"We did better than that." Gray pulled one of the photos from the stack. "We found the shooter's nest. Second floor, third window from the right, just above the flower shop. The lady who leases the shop said there were several empty rooms with back stairs access."

"Good position," McCabe commented. "He shouldn't have missed."

Roma blinked, hardly believing she'd heard right. The bluntness of McCabe's comment flicked her on the raw. "That's why all this fuss is for nothing," she said curtly, irritated at being left out of the discussion as if she had no part in it, and stung by McCabe's clinical assessment of the so-called attempt on her life. Stung by the memory of that single rifle shot. Anyone would think Lewis didn't count, despite being the one with a bullet hole in his shoulder. "If the shooter was that professional and had wanted to put a bullet through me, why did he miss?"

McCabe's gaze fastened on hers. "Your boyfriend was hit."

Roma gritted her teeth. "Lewis isn't my boyfriend, he's a friend. There was also a large crowd. Maybe the gunman was after someone else. Maybe, as you say, it was a random shooting and he didn't care who he hit."

"Anything's possible."

McCabe's voice was low, with an intriguing roughness that made her tighten up inside; then it registered that he was *soothing* her, as if she needed to be babied out of her fears.

He switched his attention back to Gray, once again dismissing her. "Calibre?"

"Five point five six."

"Sniper rifle," he said softly.

Gray glanced at Roma. She knew what he was thinking. He didn't like discussing the details of the shooting in front of her, but she wasn't going to take the hint and walk away while they discussed the unpleasant facts. Besides, she'd made it her business to find out every last detail of the investigation. In point of fact, she knew more than anyone—she had been there.

McCabe eased the photographs and the report back into the envelope. "Any fingerprints?"

"Clean." Once again Gray glanced at her as if she was made of delicate porcelain and shouldn't hear gritty details.

Roma folded her arms across her chest and almost rolled her eyes with exasperation.

"The room was sanitised before he left. Random target practice or not, he was a pro."

McCabe grunted and tapped the envelope against his thigh. "You need a lift into town?"

Gray shook his head. "I'm catching a flight out, I've got a lunchtime meeting in Sydney. The family suite at the hotel is free, so that's where you'll be staying. Roma has her itinerary, and you've got my cell phone number if you need to get hold of me."

They shook hands; then Gray hugged Roma. "I know you think this is a lot of fuss about nothing, but if there's even the suggestion of trouble, I want you back home and safe."

"You worry too much."

A wry smile tugged at the corners of his mouth. "Where you're concerned, sometimes I don't think I worry enough."

Roma watched Gray stride away, fighting the urge to call him back and cancel this whole trip. She didn't get to see much of Gray or Blade these days, and the gap in years had always precluded real intimacy, so this sudden urge to cling was definitely out of character. But now that her brother had gone there was just her and—

"Is this all your luggage?"

Roma stiffened at the grimness of McCabe's tone. One of those big calloused hands was wrapped around the handle of her suitcase. She fought the urge to snatch the case off him and wondered how he would react to the tussle. Gray would have let her have her way…eventually. She didn't think McCabe would. He hadn't openly revealed his dislike, but she could feel it rolling off him in waves.

"If I had any more luggage," she stated coolly, "I'd be carrying it."

He eyed her sharply then nodded. "When you're ready…Ms. Lombard."

She noticed he used the impersonal address of Ms.

instead of the old-fashioned but infinitely more feminine Miss.

She measured the impersonal regard of his dark blue eyes as she fell into step beside him. If there had been heat there before, it was well and truly gone. McCabe's expression was chilly, bordering on rudeness. If this was his usual manner with paying customers, she would hate to see his client list. She would bet that no one ever hired him twice. The Lombard payroll usually commanded a high level of competency, skill and politeness. She had no doubt McCabe fulfilled the first two items on that list— Gray wouldn't have hired him otherwise—but he looked as though he didn't give a damn about the third.

For the first time she registered the orange stain on his shoulder. Like the casual clothes, the stain made McCabe less machine-like and distant, more human, and it reminded her that he had a daughter and a life she knew nothing about. "Is that ice cream?" she asked, curiosity and an impish desire to put a crack in his cool reserve getting the better of her.

His gaze settled on her. "Orange chocolate chip."

Nope, Roma thought, suppressing a sigh, not a glimmer of humour.

Shifting her suitcase to his left hand, he half turned, doing a quick sweep of the Arrivals area and the people using the entrance. As he did so, his T-shirt lifted slightly and settled against a bulge in

the small of his back. A handgun. And it wasn't little—a nine millimetre would probably fit snugly into
his big, capable hand.

Roma controlled the spurt of apprehension caused
by just seeing the gun. She wasn't usually so jumpy,
but there was no getting past the fact that Lewis's
shooting had shaken her. ''I wouldn't have picked
you for a chocolate chip man.''

Chocolate chip sounded like fun.

His narrowed gaze swung back to hers. This close,
she could see the crystalline purity of his eyes, the
soft, glossy texture of his hair, the stubble darkening
his jaw. She could smell the clean scent of his skin,
as if he wasn't long from the shower. The details
were curiously intimate, and her stomach tightened
on another shot of pure sexual awareness.

''I like chocolate just as much as the next guy,''
he said evenly, ''even though it gives me one hell of
a headache.''

As they strolled toward the car park, Roma decided McCabe hadn't been talking about food. She
didn't know what chocolate had to do with anything,
but she'd been right in her first assessment: he didn't
like her. He would protect her, but only because he
was paid to do so. Somehow that burned, which was
ridiculous, because she shouldn't care whether he
liked her or not, and she didn't want to see McCabe
as anything other than a paid professional.

But with that first eye contact McCabe had made
her see him as a man, and that scared her. Men got

hurt. No matter how irritable or bad-tempered, they bled and died. She didn't want to think of McCabe bleeding the way Lewis had. Dying the way her brother Jake had.

A throb of grief hit her as she stepped from beneath the shelter of the terminal into the full glare of the sun. Blindly, Roma groped in her holdall, found her sunglasses and pushed them onto the bridge of her nose, glad for an excuse to hide the tears.

Every now and then something triggered a remnant of the intense grief, the helpless rage, she'd felt when her brother was killed. In the first weeks after Jake had died, she'd suffered recurring nightmares. She would wake, rigid with shock and distress, pillow wet with tears, then lie there, replaying the dream, trying to neutralise it by changing it, by saving Jake.

In her mind she'd saved him a hundred times, a thousand times. She'd known karate, judo; she'd been an expert shot. In her heart she'd grieved because she'd never had a chance to save him, or, like her brothers, to at least bring his killer to justice.

Lewis's shooting had brought it all back, the grief, the fear, the anger. So far she'd managed to keep her feelings firmly under wraps, shocked by the sudden eruption of violence outside the cinema and panicked by her loss of control on the sidewalk. Maybe that had been a mistake. She should have allowed herself to cry, taken the sleeping pills the doctor had prescribed so she could at least have gotten some sleep.

McCabe wouldn't appreciate having a weeping female on his hands.

Offering her a shoulder to cry on was probably right up there with shopping and cross-dressing.

Chapter 5

Ben loaded Roma's suitcase into the back of his truck. The case was another detail about Roma Lombard that didn't fit. It was leather and expensive, but it was battered. He had expected her to have a full set of Louis Vuitton, at the very least.

She didn't wait for him to open her door or to assist her into the passenger seat, for which he was thankful. He didn't want to lay one finger on his client's soft, sleek hide if he could help it. Occasionally, in the line of duty, he would have to, but he would keep those instances to a minimum. Bodyguarding required a certain distance, a sharp awareness of surroundings and clear tactical thinking, and he couldn't guarantee any of those things if he let himself get too close to Roma Lombard.

He was good at what he did; that was why he'd chosen security and VIP protection as a career option after leaving the SAS. But he also knew his own nature. He had a healthy libido and an appreciation of beautiful women. If they became intimate—and given his awareness of her as a woman, he had to anticipate that problem—he would instantly replace himself, because he would have compromised his effectiveness.

He tossed the envelope Gray had given him on the back seat of the extended cab truck, removed the Glock from the small of his back and stowed it, then swung behind the wheel and slid dark glasses onto the bridge of his nose. He opened his window to dissipate some of the heat that had built up inside. Despite the early hour, the temperature was climbing steadily. Already his T-shirt was sticking to his back, and a fine sheen of sweat dampened his skin. He was still aroused, which made sitting uncomfortable, but he kept his expression neutral. There was no point in getting wound up when he couldn't do a thing about it.

Roma was silent as he negotiated the crammed car park, her head turned away from him as she looked out the passenger window.

Ben frowned as he nosed into traffic. He'd been hard on her. He hadn't bothered to hide his dislike of a situation that had been sprung on him at the last minute. Normally he was scrupulously fair with clients, no matter what the circumstances were or who they were. Normally he was friendly.

But nothing about this situation even approached normal. The second he'd laid eyes on Roma Lombard, he'd been knocked off balance.

A welcome breeze began circulating through the overheated cab, and he caught the faint drift of a light, feminine perfume. The throb in his groin deepened into a persistent ache that told him he hadn't had sex in too long and that it was past time he took care of that particular need. He'd been too busy caring for his daughter, Bunny, and setting up his new business to look after that part of his life, but that was going to have to change. He knew from experience that ignoring his sex drive only made his state of arousal more intense. Sometimes, when he'd been on a military assignment for a prolonged period, he'd become almost savage with lust. He'd never lost control, but when he found a willing bed partner he would stay on her the entire night, keeping her beneath him and having her until the hungry ache finally left him.

A bed partner was what he needed now, a woman who could provide him with regular, hard-driving sex when he needed it and who didn't ask for anything more. Maybe it was a cold way to approach obtaining something as intimate as making love, but Ben had long since replaced romanticism with practicality. For him it was a simple physical equation, minus the hearts and flowers. When he was younger, he'd been wild, his judgement lousy. He'd let sex cloud his thinking, and the mistake had changed his life permanently. He couldn't afford to make another mistake now; he had Bunny's needs to consider. If he took a woman to bed, he was careful to lay down the ground rules first.

If, and when, he wanted a relationship of a permanent kind, it would be of *his* choosing. And this time he would choose his future wife with the contents of his head and not his pants.

He stopped for a set of lights. With the cessation of movement, the cooling breeze died and the cab instantly warmed. Roma leaned forward, the movement drawing his eye so that he watched as she reached into her holdall, extracted a bottle of water and took a swallow, before recapping and replacing the bottle. Her hands were slim, the nails short but nicely shaped, her movements graceful and completely feminine. Despite the heat and the heavier clothes she'd worn for the early-morning flight, she looked as cool as a cucumber and so composed it was hard to believe she'd saved a man's life on a bloodied sidewalk two nights ago.

The lights changed. Ben shifted gear, accelerating smoothly.

If he decided he wanted Roma Lombard, he thought calmly, then he would have her, but it was either strictly business, or bed. He couldn't protect her if he couldn't keep his mind out of her pants.

Roma avoided looking at McCabe as he drove.

Instead, she rested her head against the seat and watched the industrial areas and the housing estates flash by, letting the hum of the engine and the monotony of the view dull the throbbing in her head. Her lids drooped, the drag of sleep almost taking her under. Her eyes popped wide. She lifted her head off the headrest and forced herself to sit straighter and take an interest in the view. The thought of falling asleep in the presence of McCabe was subtly alarming; she was already vulnerable enough.

After a few minutes she noticed they were headed south into suburbia, rather than into the centre of town. Curiously she noted the signs. Gradually the houses thinned out into expensive rural lifestyle blocks, interspersed by tracts of pasture. The country was getting wilder by the second, and she wondered with a flicker of amusement if McCabe had consigned the whole idea of guarding her to the too-hard basket and was planning to knock her off and dump her body.

Eventually they turned down a gravel drive flanked by leafy jacaranda trees. There was open country on either side, where horses grazed contentedly, and in the distance, Roma caught tantalising glimpses of what must be the Waitemata Harbour.

They pulled up at a large cedar-and-brick home, which was comfortably nestled into mature gardens. A broad sweep of lawn was dominated by a large, gnarled oak. A simple rope swing hung from the oak, and a bright pink bike lay nearby, abandoned at a drunken angle next to a sandpit.

"Won't be a minute," McCabe said, placing his sunglasses on the dash and climbing out of the truck.

The front door was flung open as he walked across the lawn. A small tornado of a girl erupted from the house, yelling, "Daddy, Daddy!"

She ran full-tilt at McCabe and wrapped herself around his legs.

McCabe's back muscles flexed and bunched, shifting smoothly beneath the damp cling of his T-shirt as he swung his daughter up into his arms. He twirled her around in a circle before wrapping her close. The little girl planted a kiss on his nose, and he grinned, white teeth flashing against his stubbled jaw as he returned the favour. She giggled and tugged at his hair.

Roma watched, still punchy with tiredness, but transfixed by the change in McCabe. She'd had him pegged as tough and rude and objectionable, but right now he looked like the poster boy for fatherhood.

The little girl demanded to be let down, commandeered his hand and tugged him over to the bike, then stood, hands on hips, as McCabe went down on his haunches to put the chain back on, his movements fluid and unhurried. He looked relaxed and content, completely at home in his role as a parent. A sharp little ache started in her chest as she watched McCabe and his child together. The happy scene, the way he was with his daughter, contrasted sharply with his abrasive manner with her—intensifying the cold sense of alienation she felt in his presence, so that she sniffed, the blues hitting her full force.

She loved family, and she was already missing hers, despite their fussing; and she loved children.

She'd even trained to work with children in professional child care, but six months ago she'd quietly given up her career after a newspaper had printed a story about her family's vulnerability to terrorism. All it had taken was a couple of crank calls to her place of work and she'd been asked to leave. Roma could even understand and sympathise with her employer. If she were a parent, she wouldn't want her child to be cared for by a woman who periodically needed an armed escort, either.

She'd considered opening her own business, but not for long. The fact had been brought home to her that she *was* a potential threat to anyone who got close to her, and children were especially vulnerable. When she'd planned her career and begun training, she hadn't imagined that the situation with Harper would continue for so many years or that, as a family, they would continue to remain so vulnerable. Somehow, through it all, a part of her had held stubbornly to the idea of a fairytale ending—the elusive ideal of a normal life.

An older woman, casually dressed in jeans and an oversize shirt, strolled out of the house. Ben wiped his hands on the grass, straightened and walked toward her. The little girl didn't follow him; instead

she stared at Roma with the unabashed curiosity of
childhood and wandered over, following an invisible
zigzag path in the grass, hands shoved into her pockets.

"Hi," she said.

"Hi yourself." Roma climbed out of the truck and
crouched down to the little girl's level, relieved as
the breeze tugged at her shirt and cooled her skin.
McCabe's daughter was maybe five or six years old,
with dark hair cut into a shining bob, and eyes the
same intense blue as her dad's. She was wearing a
T-shirt, overalls and sneakers, and still had an ador-
able baby softness to her cheeks. "My name's Roma,
what's yours?"

McCabe's daughter looked back at her daddy, then
at the truck, as if assessing whether or not she should
answer. "Bunny."

She advanced a step and picked up a strand of
Roma's hair, watched it blow from her fingers. "I'd
like my hair that long," she announced. "Grandma
says I can't grow it yet. It's too fine."

"Your hair's pretty like it is."

Bunny nodded. Her eyes dropped to Roma's boots.
She gave her own grubby sneakers a disparaging
glance. "I'd like boots like that, too. But I s'pose I'll
have to wait. Grandma doesn't know what little girls
wear these days."

Roma glanced at the woman McCabe was talking
to. She was tall, with imperious features and dark
hair that had greyed in elegant streaks. The relation-

ship, even if Bunny hadn't pointed it out, was obvious. Not only did McCabe have a daughter, he had a mother.

McCabe finished his conversation and strode back toward them. Roma straightened, watching as Bunny skipped toward her father and demanded to be picked up. McCabe obliged, hardly breaking his stride.

Bunny wrapped her arms around McCabe's neck, cuddling close as she regarded Roma with the clinically assessing eyes of childhood. "She's pretty. I want her to stay."

"We both have to go, honey," McCabe said gently as he took a small suitcase from the back seat. "I have to work."

Bunny's jaw set. "I don't want you to go."

McCabe shot Roma an enigmatic look. "We've talked about my work lots of times, honey. You know I have to stay away. Grandma will look after you until I can come back, then I'll take you to the beach. We'll go camping again."

A small set of hands framed McCabe's hard face. "Promise?"

"Yeah," McCabe said softly. "Promise."

She sighed heavily. "Okay. We got a deal."

McCabe hugged her, then set her on her feet before going down on his haunches. "Look after Grandma for me?"

Bunny heaved another sigh. "I s'pose."

"And don't forget to ring, otherwise I might sleep in and be late for work."

She checked the tiny watch strapped to her wrist. "Okay. Seven 'clock. On the dot."

McCabe's mother, who had approached at an unhurried pace, came to a halt beside her son. McCabe made quick introductions before handing Elsa McCabe the suitcase, which was evidently packed with Bunny's things.

Minutes later they were heading back into suburbia.

Roma glanced at the orange stain on his T-shirt, and decided to give conversation one more try. Anything was better than McCabe's prickly silence."That's where the ice cream came from?"

He glanced at her, his gaze remote behind the dark lenses of his sunglasses. "Yeah. Bunny loves ice cream."

"Is that her real name?"

For a moment Roma thought he wasn't going to answer at all. His manner was definitely cool, withdrawn.

"Her real name's Eveline, a mouthful for a toddler. I called her honey, and she insisted that was her name, but she couldn't say the 'h.' Bunny came out instead."

The cool politeness of McCabe's reply effectively slammed the door on any more questions about his daughter. His attitude said loud and clear that she was trespassing.

Chapter 6

Ben removed his sunglasses as he turned into the underground car park of the Lombard Hotel. The huge luxury hotel and casino complex occupied a piece of prime real estate in downtown Auckland, just spitting distance from the bustling waterfront.

He killed the engine, leaned back in his seat and considered his passenger. She was slumped against the door, her head canted at an uncomfortable angle, hair tousled, her mouth even softer in sleep. For the first time he noticed the shadows beneath her eyes. She looked exhausted.

He should have offered her his shoulder. If it had been any other woman, he would have. He was naturally protective, and he liked looking after women. He loved their soft skin and silky hair, the graceful

things they did with their hands, all the differences
that made them female. The problem was, Roma
Lombard was too tempting. If she'd slept on his
shoulder, he would have been too aware of her.

He was going to have to wake her, and he didn't
want to; she needed to sleep. An unexpected wave
of tenderness took him by surprise, and he drew back
from it, instantly wary. He'd already gotten way too
close to his client; he wasn't about to step any closer
if he could help it. Especially not after he'd turned
around and seen Bunny holding a strand of her hair
and looking at her as if she were a fairy princess out
of one of her books. They'd looked like mother and
daughter, and warning bells had gone off inside him.

He never brought women home to Bunny, because
she'd made it clear she wanted a mother and Ben
didn't want her fixating on a woman who might
never fill the job. She'd had enough instability in her
life; he would be damned if he'd introduce any more.
When he'd finally gotten full custody just months
ago, he'd vowed to do all he could to make up for
the upheaval of the marriage split and give her a
settled childhood.

He called Roma's name. When she didn't respond,
he reached out and shook her lightly. She stirred but
didn't waken. Reluctantly, he gripped her shoulder
again, noting the sleek firmness of muscle beneath
his hand, and shook a bit harder.

Roma came out of sleep fast, the abrupt transition
from a deep, fathomless slumber to alarmed wake-

fulness making her heart pound and her breath catch in her throat. For a raw moment she was trapped in a disorienting limbo, caught between dream and reality, the darkness of her surroundings making fear rise in her throat, until she recognised the dim, bunker-like surrounds of the hotel's underground car park.

"You okay?"

McCabe's dark, clipped voice brought her head up with a jerk. Pain shafted up her neck and made the tender spot where she'd hit her head on the sidewalk outside the cinema throb. She blinked and rubbed at her eyes, gradually coming to grips with the embarrassing knowledge that she had fallen asleep while McCabe had been driving and had probably been asleep for a good half hour in his presence. She massaged her neck, tested the kink there with a turn of her head, then reluctantly glanced at the big grim man sitting beside her. "Fine. Just a little…startled."

McCabe regarded her for a moment longer, giving her the impression that he was going to say something more; then he climbed out of the truck and walked around to the rear to get her case.

They picked up the keys from reception and took the lift up to the Lombard family suite. McCabe dropped her bag just inside the door, did a quick tour of the rooms, then came back into the main lounge area.

Roma had already done her own tour of the room she wanted—one of the big airy double rooms with bifold doors that opened out onto a sun-dappled terrace. It was the room she always had when she could grab it. Of course, that depended on how many of her family were in residence. Sometimes the place was a zoo and she'd had to fight for a single bed in the smallest room.

McCabe strolled into the lounge and motioned to one of the comfortable leather couches grouped around a coffee table. "I know you probably want to take a nap, but before you do that, we need to talk."

Roma's stomach tightened at the curtness of McCabe's tone, and the fact that she had to share the suite with a man who was little more than a stranger for the next few days hit her forcibly. She had only ever been in this situation with a bodyguard a couple of times, and she couldn't be comfortable with the necessity. Usually there was family around to act as a buffer against the reality of around-the-clock protection.

She sat down on one of the big, soft hide couches that dominated the lounge and mentally braced herself for McCabe's list of rules. Gray had said the security would be discreet, but that meant to outside observers only—it had nothing to do with the impact the protection would have on her own life.

McCabe perched on the arm of the couch directly

opposite. "I want to know your version of what happened with the shooting."

For a moment Roma's mind went blank, and she wondered if she'd heard right. This wasn't the discussion she had expected.

"I gave my version to the police. All the relevant facts are in the report Gray gave you."

"I know the facts," he said calmly. "What I want from you are the things you might not have told the police." His gaze fastened on hers, dark and still, giving the impression of utter coldness. "Were you scared when it happened?"

"What do you think?" she demanded quietly. "Lewis was hurt, and there was the possibility of a second shot. I was so scared all I wanted to do was run."

"But you didn't. You stayed and gave your friend first aid."

"He was bleeding. If I'd left him, he would have died."

He crossed his arms over his chest, his expression neutral, cop-cool. "Did you think the shooting was random?"

"There's no proof it was anything else."

He was silent for a moment. "You were scared when I woke you in the Jeep. Would you mind telling me why?"

Resentment stirred. Not only did McCabe look like a cop, he was questioning her like one. "I woke up in an unfamiliar place. I was…off balance."

"If you have information about the shooting that I should know," he said softly, "you'd better tell me. I can't do my job effectively unless I know all the facts."

The sluggish aftermath of her nap and the odd sense of disconnection that went with it evaporated on a hot rush of anger. McCabe thought she was withholding information. Lying. More…he was interrogating her as if she were a suspect in the shooting, not a victim. "I don't know anything about the shooting other than that the person I was with got hurt," she snapped. "Everything there is to know is included in the report in that envelope."

Keeping her expression carefully blank, Roma stood up and collected her case, strode toward her room and dumped the case just inside the door. Too angry to leave the conversation hanging, she spun on her heel and almost ran into McCabe's chest. She stared at the sleek gold skin of his throat and the pulse that jumped there, trying to steady the hard pounding of her heart. "What made you think I might know anything more?"

"You were scared when you woke up. And you're evasive now. I need to know why. I have staff who'll be involved in your protection programme. Their safety's important. I have to check out all the angles."

All the angles. She took a deep breath, every nerve in her body jangling at his closeness. He was blocking the doorway now, one hand resting on the jamb, muscled bicep gleaming in the sunny glow of the room.

Hurt and resentment warred with common sense. Common sense won out. He was doing his job, asking the questions he had to ask. But if he'd been nicer about it, explained what he was doing, there wouldn't have been a problem. She would have been happy to discuss the shooting with him. "I panicked while I was giving Lewis first aid," she said flatly. "I'm not proud of it, but for a few seconds I did think I was being watched. I did think I was a target." She met his gaze squarely. "I didn't put that in the police report for a good reason. It was paranoia, pure and simple."

"I'm sorry if I offended you, but you were so jumpy I had to find out if you felt directly threatened." He shrugged. "Gray doesn't think there's a threat, but given your family's past history, he's not taking any chances. I'm not taking any chances, either." His voice had dropped, the low, rough register making her tighten up inside. "If at any point you feel that someone is after you, then tell me. It'll make a difference to the way I protect you."

Roma eyed him warily. He'd used that same dark, honeyed tone at the airport. It was probably the one he used for escaped mental patients. Or for seducing women. Warmth spread through her at the thought of being seduced by McCabe. "What if it turns out to be my overactive imagination?"

''It wouldn't matter. As long as the protection makes you feel safe.''

The concern in McCabe's voice startled her, and she wondered if he was actually on the verge of offering her comfort. His face was half in shadow, half out of it, wide mouth distractingly soft, set as it was against the square line of his jaw. His scent filled her nostrils, musky and hot in the warm room.

He was aroused.

The shock of the discovery sent a spasm of heat through her stomach, tightening her nipples in a rush, so that they pushed achingly hard against the soft cotton of her bra. For a long moment, time seemed to stop, become suspended, along with her breathing, while she struggled with that knowledge.

Awareness flashed in those cold wolf's eyes, shivered down her spine. He held her gaze, seemingly unconcerned that she knew he was aroused.

One part of her wanted to back up a step, confused. After all, they'd been fighting on and off ever since they'd met. But another part of her was irresistibly drawn, attracted and curious. She wondered what it would be like to step up to McCabe and rub herself against him, bury her face in the curve of his neck and taste his skin, wind her fingers in his hair, then reach up and press her mouth against his.

A little shudder ran through her. Dangerous, she decided.

Her brothers had been wild when they'd been single, and they'd run with a wild bunch. Apart from his brief marriage, McCabe had always been in there.

"Did you tell Gray how you felt about the shooting?"

For a moment Roma had trouble grasping that, despite his sexual arousal, McCabe had coldly switched to bodyguard mode and wanted to talk about the shooting again.

"He knew I was scared."

Ben studied Roma's expression, the defensive way she clasped her arms across her chest to hide the jut of her nipples. Her breasts were round and full against her slim figure. The contrast of feminine lushness with sleek, firm muscle made his mouth water. He wanted to reach out now and cup her breasts, weigh them in his palms, rub his thumbs over her tight little nipples, then have them in his mouth. The mere thought of having her naked breasts in his hands, then sucking her nipples until she moaned, made him achingly hard.

Not that anything like that was about to happen. He was already walking a knife's edge with his client, and when she heard what he was about to say, it was more likely she would slug him than allow him to touch her in any way.

"There's just one more thing," he said softly. "You can't have that room."

Her eyes narrowed. McCabe watched her closely, reluctantly fascinated by every nuance of expression. He knew Roma's brothers as well as if they were his own family. Gray and Blade were both big, male, muscled—capable of pounding most other men into the dirt without breaking a sweat. Not that they brawled; they didn't need to. Gray and Blade had always fought with intellect and technical skill as much as with the physical power of their bodies; they were warriors in every sense of the word.

Idly, he wondered how Roma would fight. Dirty, he decided—suppressing a grin. He could see her temper now, simmering just below the surface. Her skin had taken on a luminous glow, and her eyes flashed, dark and slumbrously exotic, as if she would go for the kill in a deceptively lazy feminine way that would flummox most men. They wouldn't know she'd sunk the knife in until hours later, maybe days.

Then again, maybe not...

Suddenly he could see the resemblance to her brothers in her cheekbones, the strength in the line of her jaw, that fierce Lombard pride.

His lids lowered. No, Roma Lombard wouldn't bother with manipulation or veiled insults, or even that female version of brawling, a sissy slap. An unholy excitement pulsed through him. She would just out and out slug him.

She didn't bother to hide her incredulity. "Did you just say," she said slowly, "that I can't have this room?"

"You heard right."

"Which room *can* I have?" she enquired with icy politeness.

He felt like saying "Mine" but pulled back from that precipice. "You can have the one through the adjoining bathroom. It's more secure. This bedroom's wide open in terms of access, with the terrace doors, and the doors leading into the bathroom and living area."

For long seconds she didn't move, didn't respond in any way, but instead of exploding as he expected her to, her expression smoothed out, becoming as controlled and remote as it had been at the airport. "All right."

She met his gaze coolly, although her cheeks were flushed, then astounded him by running her gaze down over his chest, his belly, stopping at his groin. He felt as though she'd just run her hand over him.

She flushed a deeper colour but didn't say a word, simply bent with smooth grace and picked up her case—beating him to it—then turned neatly on her heel and strolled through the bathroom into the adjoining bedroom. He heard the gentle click of the door as she closed it.

Her easy agreement, the cool way she'd just looked him over and dismissed him, made McCabe go utterly still inside, all his attention focused sharply on what had just happened. She hadn't liked being ordered to take another room, but she'd weighed the options and accepted his logic. The extent of her control was impressive, the silent battle over so swiftly that if he'd blinked, he would have missed it.

Not many people surprised him: Roma Lombard

just had. He'd been ready to read her the riot act, sure she was going to give him the runaround. His own temper had been on a hair trigger despite his arousal and amusement; then, with two words and the elegant line of her back, she'd dismissed him. It was a neat trick.

He felt like kicking himself. He'd made the mistake of basing his opinion of her on what he'd heard from her brothers, but the woman he was dealing with was nothing like the kid sister Gray and Blade had told stories about. He began to see how she'd run rings around so many security professionals in the past. They'd all been bamboozled by her dainty figure, that pretty face, those exotic eyes.

Her understated femininity, that touch-me-not remoteness, was just the first layer of deception.

He knew she'd operated under fire, because that was effectively what she'd done when she'd saved Lewis Harrington's life two nights ago. There was nothing lightweight or childlike about Roma Lombard's courage.

He wondered how many more layers he would uncover before he hit bedrock, or what the bedrock comprised. He had a feeling the lady had uncharted depths.

The attraction he felt sharpened, deepened. The last time he'd felt anything remotely like this, he'd ended up married.

That thought stopped him in his tracks.

Ben turned from the bedroom and surveyed the

lounge, barely seeing any of the comfortable furnishings, the well-stocked bookshelves, the state-of-the-art stereo system, the sunlight that shafted into the room, bouncing off glossy wood floors.

Coldly, he examined exactly what he was feeling.

Roma Lombard was attractive and utterly female, with an edge to her that he found irresistible, but it was more than that. She aroused him on some primitive, physical level he couldn't explain. He'd taken one look at her and gotten hard.

He was still hard, but if that had been the extent of the attraction, he could have ignored it. The problem was that he was attracted, period.

That remote, self-contained quality intrigued and tantalised him. It wouldn't be enough to simply have her naked beneath him in bed, those dark eyes locked with his while he pushed inside her. He wanted to batter down her defences and find out all the things she was hiding from him, what made her laugh and what made her cry, what she liked to eat, what movies she liked to watch. He wanted her soft and clinging in his arms, and he wanted to know what she sounded like when she came.

Oh, yeah, he was in trouble.

When he'd read the police report Gray had given him, he'd understood why Gray had wanted him. Roma had been through a traumatic experience. She was vulnerable, whether she was prepared to admit it or not, and she needed more than simple bodyguarding. She needed comforting, babying. Normally, he was good for that.

His jaw tightened. He didn't have to wonder how Gray and Blade would react if they ever found out he wanted to do a lot more than just lend their sister a shoulder to cry on. They wouldn't bother with conversation. They would draw straws to see who got to beat the living hell out of him first.

He was beginning to think it might be worth it.

Chapter 7

Roma lifted her case onto the bed, unzipped it and began unpacking. Doggedly, she shook out clothes and put them on hangers, aligned her shoes in the wardrobe, and stacked underwear and T-shirts in the dresser that sat to one side of the queen-size bed—using the ritual of establishing her presence in the room to soothe her shattered nerves.

The room itself was comfortable, with a ceiling fan slowly circulating the air and homey little touches. One of Aunt Sophie's cheerful watercolours was affixed to one wall, and a bowl piled with shells sat on top of the dresser, striking a beachy note.

She touched a fingertip to the nubby sage green of a kina shell, a sea egg, which had probably been collected by one of her beachcombing cousins, a smile curving her mouth at the familiar, quirky evidence of her family.

She stacked toiletries in the bathroom and on impulse examined the bottle of sleeping pills, shook one out, poured herself a glass of water, then carried the pill and the water into the bedroom and set them down on the bedside table.

Her mood changed abruptly when she locked the two doors of the room, emptied her make-up case, placing the items neatly on the dressing table, then removed the false bottom of the case. The compartment held a Sig Sauer P-226, complete with a laser sighting system, a magazine and a box of ammunition, all secured with masking tape to avoid movement or damage during transit. Gray would have a fit if he knew she'd brought her gun with her; she'd broken the law just carrying it into the country, but she'd felt too shaky to leave without it.

As security blankets went, it wasn't much, but those moments outside the cinema had stripped another layer of innocence from her. Whether she ever used the gun or not was immaterial; just the fact that she had the means to defend herself made her feel more in control.

She peeled tape off, pulled the Sig out and wiped it clean of any sticky residue with the cloth and cleaning fluid packed in with the gun. As handguns went, the Sig wasn't pretty, but it was sturdy, all black—all business—the steel dull, the textured wooden grip plate practical. Primarily a military weapon, it had the advantage of being lighter than a lot of sporting pistols on the market, and it was more basic, easier to break down. She didn't win any prizes shooting at her gun club when put against some of the fancy custom-made pieces some of the members used, but for Roma that wasn't an issue. She simply needed to be armed with a gun that was reliable, and she needed to be familiar enough with that gun that she was confident handling it in an emergency.

With methodical movements, she placed the Sig on the dresser, peeled tape off the magazine, wiped that down and slotted shells into it, leaving the load short one round to lessen the possibility of jamming. She slid the magazine into place, checking that the action was smooth, then critically examined the gun. If she was going to carry it with her, she would have to lessen some of the bulk. The laser sight would have to go.

Setting it down, she removed the magazine and rummaged in her holdall for her case of tools, then carried everything over to the bed. The laser transmitter was mounted on a bracket, which was screwed onto the barrel, and a connecting cord ran from the laser down to the hand grip, where the control button that triggered the system was affixed. She would have to unscrew the grip plate of the gun to remove the control pad, then take the bracket off the barrel to dismantle the system. Flipping open the tool case, she selected a screwdriver.

When she was finished, Roma shoved the magazine back into the housing, stood and levelled the gun, two-handed, adjusting to the changed weight. Without the sight the Sig was lighter, the balance different, less unwieldy. She would no longer have the advantage of precision targeting, but that wasn't such a big deal. She didn't often use the laser targetting anyway, preferring to build her skill by acquiring her targets manually, and this way it would fit better into her holdall or handbag.

The thought that she might actually have to use the gun wasn't a welcome one. Lewis's injury had brought home to her just how horrifying the damage could be, and she didn't want to inflict that kind of wound on anyone, not even a killer. But she would if she had to. Kneeling over Lewis on that sidewalk had changed her in some basic way. She didn't like guns or the necessity of an armed escort, but danger or not, never again would she leave herself so open and vulnerable.

Checking that the safety was on, she slipped the gun into her holdall and folded a sweatshirt around it to make sure that nothing could bump against the safety switch and accidentally enable the gun. When she was satisfied the gun was safe, she stowed the bag in the wardrobe, slipped off her boots and lay down on the bed.

Minutes ticked by as she lay staring at the ceiling and the slow stirring of the fan as it moved tepid air around the room. Apart from the occasional sound of the telephone and the low register of McCabe's voice when he answered it, the suite was quiet, the hum of the city distant.

Memory drifted back like awkward pieces of flotsam: the airport, McCabe, McCabe's daughter, Bunny. Other unwanted images crowded on the heels of that basic recall. Handling the gun had made her tense and restless. No matter how much she'd prepared herself for violence over the years, her mind had never adjusted to the reality of it.

Frustration pulled at her. The headache was still there, dull and persistent, and her eyes felt gritty, but she was wound up too tight to relax.

Reluctantly, she propped herself up on one elbow and picked up the sleeping pill. The only other times she'd taken them had been after Jake's death, and again when Gray and Sam had been held hostage.

She didn't like taking pills, didn't like relinquishing one bit of control, but she couldn't function much longer without sleep.

She slipped the pill into her mouth, took a swallow of water, then settled back to wait, staring blankly at the ceiling.

Ben called up a file on his laptop and began checking the security specs of the hotel, and of this suite in particular. He was already familiar with some of the details, because he'd visited this suite before, when Blade was in residence.

Frowning, he checked his watch. It was late after-

noon, and Roma still hadn't woken up. During the
time she'd spent sleeping, Ben had retrieved his own
packed case from the Jeep, showered and changed
into clean clothes, eaten lunch and taken a quick cat-
nap.

The phone rang. It was the guy who'd rung twice
earlier—light, honeyed baritone, hell of a vocabu-
lary, a real smooth bastard. Evan diVaggio.

"She's still sleeping," Ben answered calmly.

"She'll want to talk to me."

The blunt pronouncement made Ben's hackles
rise. He sat back in his chair and coolly considered
his caller. "I've got your number. She'll ring you
when she wakes up."

DiVaggio kept talking, evidently unused to taking
no for an answer. Ben listened without comment, not
bothering to take notes. He had enough problems
with this job as it was. The hell he would be Roma
Lombard's social secretary. After hanging up, he
phoned reception and asked them to hold all calls
until further notice.

Four hours later, Roma still hadn't stirred and Ben
was worried.

He knocked on her door, which opened out into
the lounge. When there was no reply, he knocked
more forcefully. Silence. He tried the door; it was
locked. He strode through his room, into the bathroom, and tried that door, then swore beneath his
breath, his patience gone. She'd locked that one, too.

He called her name. No answer. Abruptly, his irritation changed to concern.

He couldn't hear anything, hadn't heard anything for hours. Now the absence of sound bothered him. Roma had been tired enough to fall asleep on the drive to the hotel, but he also acknowledged she was an unknown quantity. He dismissed the possibility that she could have left the suite while he was collecting his bag from the truck or having a shower, because both doors were locked from the inside, and besides, she wouldn't leave without telling him, no matter how much she objected to the security arrangements. There were two possibilities. She could simply be sleeping very heavily, or she could be ill. Ben knocked once more and called her name. When there was still no reply, he stepped back, calmly considering his next move...and saw the bottle of pills.

He examined the label and frowned. Sleeping pills. He unscrewed the cap and shook a few out onto his palm. There weren't many, but he had no way of knowing how many pills had been in the bottle, or how many she'd taken.

Slipping the small bottle into his pocket, he strode out and rummaged through one of the bags of security gear he'd had delivered that afternoon and extracted his tool kit. Minutes later, with the aid of a small screwdriver, he'd dismantled the lock on the bathroom door and pushed it wide.

She was lying, fully clothed on top of the bed,

curled up on her side, her shirt twisted slightly, her feet bare.

Ben said her name, his voice startlingly loud in the dim room. When she didn't respond, he walked over to the bed and shook her shoulder. She stirred, her eyes barely flickering before she sank back into sleep.

He shook her shoulder again and when there was no response he went down on his haunches beside the bed, picked up her wrist and measured her pulse. It was normal.

Ben assessed the situation. She probably hadn't had much sleep since the shooting. Adrenaline and shock could do that to you. He'd seen guys in combat, jittery with nerves for days after they'd had an enemy contact. But there was also the possibility she'd taken too many pills. He didn't think so, but he wasn't about to dismiss that possibility out of hand.

His decision made, he sat on the side of the bed and lifted her into a sitting position, supporting her with one arm around her shoulders. Her head bumped his chin, nestled against his shoulder; dark, silky hair slid over his arm, making him tense. She was warm and pliant against him, and the light female scent of her rose up, teasing at his nostrils. "Come on, honey," he muttered, *"Wake up."*

The demand in the dark male voice finally penetrated the thick fog of sleep that wrapped Roma as cosily as a soft wool blanket. She tried to turn away from the voice, but when she found she couldn't, settled for staying where she was, nuzzling into the warm, solid, *ungiving* pillow and wondering if she was caught in one of those peculiar dreams that take on the trappings of reality: heat, touch, sound…scent.

The scent clung in her mind when everything else drifted away. She breathed in more deeply, automatically trying to identify the separate components. The scents were pleasing, masculine…. Clean skin and soap, a faint resinous bite of cologne…just enough to tease.

For a moment she was blank, her mind still essentially closed down, body relaxed into the slackness of sleep. Then awareness hit. Her eyes popped open and fastened on the lean dark face so close to her own. McCabe.

His arm was wrapped around her shoulders, supporting her in a sitting position. She was surrounded by him, practically in his lap. One big hand cupped her chin, tilting her head back against the warm hollow of his shoulder, the pads of his fingers rough against her skin. Heat radiated from him, burned her with an electrical tingle wherever his bare skin touched hers, but his gaze was cool, clinical.

"What is it?" she said, her voice husky from sleep. "What's wrong?"

He released her and stood, digging a bottle out of his pocket. "These."

Her sleeping pills.

"How many did you take?"

Roma was abruptly aware of the dimness of the room, the sense that a great deal of time had passed. She checked her wristwatch and saw with a sense of shock that she'd slept the entire day away. The insomnia and that one sleeping pill had knocked her sideways. Swinging her legs over the side of the bed, she stood, still feeling woozy, and remembered that she hadn't eaten all day. "One pill, that's all I took." She let out a disgusted breath. "The last one I'll ever take."

"Good." His fingers closed around the bottle. "Because I'm throwing them away. And there's one more thing we need to discuss. You'd better lose the fortress mentality fast. When you didn't respond, I had to unlock the door with a screwdriver to get to you." His voice was calm, neutral, but there was an underlying coldness that made her stiffen. "Don't lock the doors against me again. Maybe you don't think you need a bodyguard. That issue is irrelevant, because you have one. If you're going to fight me on standard safety precautions, this isn't going to work. I want you to admit the possibility that there is a threat, no matter how remote, and let me do my job."

Her chin shot up and heat surged into her cheeks, burning away the drowsiness as she met McCabe's gaze. He'd changed into a black T-shirt and black pants, and in the shadowed room the clean-cut angles of his face seemed even more harshly honed, his eyes hooded, the scar more prominent. Not for the first time, she wondered how he'd come by the slice on his cheekbone. She decided it was entirely possible that a woman had done it.

McCabe believed she'd locked the doors against him. Well, she had, but only so she could conceal the fact that she had a gun. She'd simply forgotten to unlock the doors before she'd gone to sleep. She wondered why he hadn't continued the interrogation by asking her *why* she'd locked the doors, but apparently he didn't need clarity on that point. Maybe he expected her to be rabbit-scared and lock her room against him like a terrified spinster, or maybe he thought she was so traumatised by the shooting that she had to barricade herself in her room, crawl under the bed and hide.

"I won't lock the doors again," she said flatly. "And I do accept the possibility of danger."

"But you're not taking it seriously."

Roma took a deep breath and did a quick count to ten. The tactic worked, just. Lewis's shooting, the years of fear when Harper had stalked her family, sat hard and cold and unresolved inside her. For all her reluctance to have a bodyguard, it had never been because she'd denied the possibility of danger. She simply wanted to live a normal life, not the half life she'd had forced upon her by a series of security crises. Whenever possible she tried to walk away from it all and just *be.* Hard to explain to a security professional. McCabe's world was black and white, his purpose easily defined: to protect. "Oh, I take it seriously. Ever since I was fifteen."

McCabe's gaze locked with hers, darkly glittering in the dim room. It took a moment to register that even though his expression hadn't changed, the way he regarded her had.

"I'm sorry," he said in a low, rough voice. "I keep forgetting what you've been through."

Something kicked hard and deep inside her. Her breath came in on a rush, as every nerve ending in her body sprang to sharp, tingling life. McCabe hadn't stepped closer, hadn't moved on her in any way, but she was suddenly unbearably aware of the intimacy of having him in her room.

A phone rang, the low buzz jolting.

McCabe said something beneath his breath, slid a cell phone from his pocket, flipped it open and put it to his ear, his gaze still fixed on her in a way that made her heart pound. After a few curt words, he abruptly turned away, strode from the room and continued the conversation out in the lounge.

Roma sank back onto the edge of the bed. Something had happened.

Her heart was hammering, and she felt odd, unsettled, as if she'd just run a race or fought a battle—and the result was still in the balance.

She wrapped her arms around her waist, hugging herself against the strangeness of her feelings. McCabe didn't like her. They didn't like each other. They'd spent all their time fighting and yet the pull of attraction was there, so strong sometimes that it threatened to knock her off her feet. It was alien territory for Roma. She'd always imagined that when she fell in love it would be sweeter, gentler.

She stopped. Whoa... Back up a step.

She wasn't in love. In lust, maybe, although she didn't accept that, either. Old-fashioned or not, casual sex was something she shied away from, although she didn't require the permission of marriage. If she'd ever fallen in love with any of her ex-boyfriends she wouldn't have been coy, she would have gone to bed with him, but that had never happened. All around her people she knew were settling into marriages, having babies, but Roma had never come close to falling in love or had a relationship that had in any way approached permanency.

The same restless dissatisfaction that had had her picking up the phone two nights ago and ringing Lewis gripped her. She'd been tired of being alone, and she'd wanted to go out. Lewis was a safe escort and good company, but that hadn't been enough. She'd wanted what every other healthy, red-blooded woman out on the prowl on a Saturday night wanted: to find her man. It was basic and primitive. She was tired of being alone; she wanted to be loved, and she wanted to make love. She wanted to know what it was like to sleep with her man, to have him on top of her while she wrapped her legs around him and took him inside her. She wanted to rub herself against him, wallow in the different textures of skin and hair, run her hands over the muscular width of his back and glory in his male strength.

She wasn't naive; she knew that sex could be hot and sweaty and messy, maybe even painful the first time. She didn't care; she wanted it.

For the first time she faced the fact that it might happen with McCabe.

She sat, her spine rigid, wondering if she was going crazy. She'd done nothing but draw battle lines with McCabe, and now she was considering sleeping with him.

She remembered what it had been like to wake up in his arms, the solid, muscular wall of his chest, the hot maleness of him, and she swallowed. She'd liked it. More than liked it. Which put her in a whole mess of trouble.

The next week wasn't going to be easy. *McCabe* wasn't going to be easy. But she would get through it. She would figure her way through the confusing minefield of being attracted to her bodyguard, endure his impatience and his restrictions, providing they weren't too intrusive. After all, Ben McCabe was just an ordinary, mortal man; he didn't have super powers.

On impulse, Roma retrieved her holdall from the wardrobe and checked that her gun was still nestled in the folds of her sweatshirt. Her fingers closed around cold metal, and she let out a relieved breath.

If McCabe had X-ray vision and found her gun, she was sunk.

Chapter 8

Ben sat down at the roomy desk that occupied a recessed area of the lounge and called up a file on his laptop.

When Roma came out, he would see about ordering dinner in; then they were going to have to sit down and go through her itinerary. From what Gray had told him over the phone, Ben knew he wasn't going to like it one little bit. But as he called up street maps and the personnel he might need to use, his mind definitely wasn't on his job.

He sat back in his chair, thoughtful. He couldn't forget the stark look in Roma Lombard's eyes, the flatness in her voice, when she'd said she took the threat seriously.

He'd wanted to continue the conversation, probe

a little more deeply, but the phone had rung. Now he wished he'd ignored the call.

All the years he'd known Gray and Blade, admittedly, mostly in a military setting, he'd been aware of how much the need to defend their family from terrorist threats had moulded their personalities. Gray had become grim and silent, Blade had just got wilder—but they'd both shared one common trait; they'd both become formidable forces in the shadowy world of undercover operations. They'd fought and trained, risen through the ranks on the strength of their natural skill in battle and a cold, incisive, intelligence, behind it all a single-minded, driving purpose. They'd hunted Egan Harper down, and in the process destroyed an entire terrorist network.

Roma Lombard was their sister.

She'd lived through those years of terrorist threat just as Gray and Blade had, the only difference was that she'd stayed at home.

He'd thought earlier on, when she was on the verge of losing her temper, how like her brothers she was. Now he had to accept that those years of living under siege had also moulded her, given her the kind of edge and courage that was unexpected in a woman who was so essentially graceful and feminine.

Then there was the other problem, the uncomfortable fact that he was having trouble keeping his hands off his client.

He kept seeing the dazed expression on her face when she'd first woken up, the way her hair had tumbled around her cheeks. She'd looked sleepy and vulnerable, and he'd wanted to slide into bed with her.

He was still aroused just thinking about how close he'd come to sinking his mouth down onto hers and backing her up to that rumpled bed. She was small against him, her skin so smooth and baby-soft, it would mark easily. Primitive heat flared through him when he considered how much he wanted to mark her as his. When he got her beneath him, he would have to be careful.

And he had no doubt that he would have her beneath him; it was only a matter of when. But as badly as he wanted her now, he would have to wait; the job came first.

Half an hour later Roma walked out into the lounge. She'd showered, washed and dried her hair, and changed into a pair of dark pants and a sleeveless knit top in her favourite deep red. She felt almost human after eating the muesli bar she'd discovered stashed in the side pocket of her holdall.

Ben was working at the corner desk, a laptop open in front of him, a security monitor set up next to the lap top—the screen split into four sections showing the entrance and exit to the private elevator, the interior of the elevator, and the door to the suite. As she walked toward him, he stretched his arms over his head, a lazy movement that made all the muscles along his back and shoulders ripple and flex beneath the soft cling of black interlock.

When he saw her, he got to his feet, propped his hips against the desk and folded his arms across his chest. "You look steadier. You'll feel even better when you've had some dinner."

Roma went still. Something was different about McCabe. His tone was mild, his expression still neutral, so that she had difficulty pinning down exactly what had changed. "Did Evan call?"

"Several times."

"Did he leave a message?"

"Just a number. But before you call anyone, we need to get some ground rules sorted out."

McCabe indicated that she should take the chair he'd been using while he worked. His manner was still neutral, relaxed. Roma sat down and crossed her legs, inching the chair back enough that she didn't feel so overwhelmed by his physical presence. And then the change in McCabe hit her. Sometime between the scene in the bedroom and the moment she walked into the lounge, McCabe's attitude had softened. She wouldn't go so far as to say he liked her, but the dislike was no longer evident.

"Gray wanted me on this job because he knows I specialise in VIP protection, not conventional bodyguarding, and he wanted the security to be discreet enough not to capture media attention. If you were a high-ranking politician, I'd look like your aide. If you were a valuable executive of a multinational corporation, I'd look like your personal assistant. Neither of those approaches will work in your case. The most obvious cover is for me to look like someone who has every right to be with you twenty-four hours a day.''

She blinked, startled, hardly believing she'd heard right. ''You mean you're going to pose as my boyfriend?''

He shrugged. ''I could pose as a friend of the family, but the fact that I'm sharing accommodation with you messes that one up. Do you have a problem with the boyfriend scenario?''

Roma could think of any number of problems, the first one being that, physical attraction aside, she couldn't imagine McCabe in the role. ''No,'' she said wryly, ''no problem.''

''Is anyone likely to object?''

''If you mean, do I have a boyfriend, the answer is no.''

''What about diVaggio?''

For a bare second Roma was confused; then she realised what he was asking. Heat rose in her at the implication. ''I'm not sleeping with Evan, if that's what you're asking.''

The phone buzzed. McCabe answered it, then held the receiver out to her. ''Speak of the devil,'' he murmured. ''Looks like diVaggio wants to come up.''

Minutes later there was a staccato rap at the door.

Ben had already surveyed the monitor as diVaggio had his ID checked by hotel security before being escorted up to the suite, and he'd had plenty of time to make his evaluations.

DiVaggio was tall, broad-shouldered, his face saved from classical male beauty by a hard-ass jaw and a nose that looked as if it had been broken playing football. Rough edges aside, the man wasn't so much smooth as slick as polished steel, with a leanly muscled physique encased in a suit that had probably cost the budget of a small third world country.

Roma flung the door open, said diVaggio's name, delight in her voice, and walked straight into his arms. DiVaggio grinned, picked her up and hugged her to his chest as he stepped into the suite.

Ben's eyes narrowed at the intimacy inherent in that simple action, the low register of diVaggio's voice as he expressed his concern about the shooting.

His irritation smouldered into temper when diVaggio took his time letting Roma go. He'd been prepared for the man to be physically unimpressive. He didn't like it at all that the guy exuded a tough strength that would garner him a lot of personal space in any company.

He liked it even less that Roma had walked into his arms so naturally. She'd said she wasn't sleeping with diVaggio. What he should have asked was had she ever slept with him. If diVaggio saw Roma as his to protect, there was going to be trouble.

Roma pulled free of diVaggio's embrace but kept hold of his arm as she turned toward Ben, grinning.

Suddenly Roma Lombard wasn't quiet or understated, she was a knockout.

Ben felt as though he'd just been kicked in the stomach. The attraction he'd so cold-bloodedly registered was obliterated by something hotter, more uncontrolled.

He took diVaggio's hand as Roma made the introductions, the shake brief, the squeeze firm, eye contact measuring. Ben decided that, in other circumstances, he could have liked the man.

"I've heard Gray talk about you," diVaggio said. "You're Special Air Service."

"Ex," Ben corrected. "I run a security firm now."

DiVaggio glanced sharply at Roma. "There's a problem?"

Ben cut in before Roma could answer. "The protection is precautionary. It'll be discreet." He held diVaggio's gaze, his own deliberately cool because he was delivering a message and he didn't want any misunderstandings. "If anyone wants to know, I'm not Roma's bodyguard, I'm her escort."

"Which means I should keep my hands off." DiVaggio's eyes narrowed. "You may as well play the bodyguard, the part sounds the same."

"In my experience, it's not a lot different."

Satisfaction filled him at the subtle retreat in diVaggio's cold gaze. Ben had staked his claim, and the other man was aware of it.

"If you've both finished marking out territory,"

Roma said, picking her holdall up off the couch and sliding the strap onto her shoulder, "shall we decide on dinner? If I don't eat soon, you won't have anything left to guard."

Chapter 9

Dinner wasn't as strained as Roma had thought it would be. A bar occupied one end of the room, and most of the tables were filled, so there was a lively buzz of conversation to fill in the silences, as well as the distraction of steady traffic between tables. The conversation naturally centred around Evan's fund-raising events. McCabe seemed content to let Evan talk, occasionally cutting in with a question about location and possible security problems.

The evening finally wound down, and Evan left. McCabe held her chair, surprising her; then she remembered that in public he was acting as her escort. As she hitched her holdall over her shoulder, she noticed two women at the next table, both with their chins propped on their hands, wineglasses in front of them, as they gazed, bemused, at McCabe.

She didn't blame them for looking. Before leaving the suite, McCabe had shrugged into a shoulder holster, then pulled a black jacket over top. The effect was stark and sexy. He wasn't slickly urbane like Evan, he was bluntly male—more man in every way—and there wasn't one woman in the restaurant who hadn't acknowledged that fact with a long sideways look.

One of the women caught her eye and grinned. "Where did you get him?"

Roma shot McCabe a sideways look. "Actually, my brother got him for me."

"Oh," she said on a sigh, "you've got a nice family."

The other woman focused on Roma. "Is he Italian?" she asked wistfully. "He looks Italian. You've gotta watch them, they're fast."

McCabe's hand landed on the small of Roma's back, sending a spasm of heat through her that made her stomach muscles contract. "In that case, I'm the one who's in trouble. She's the Italian, not me."

The woman blinked, riveted by McCabe's deep, raspy voice. "In this case," she said judiciously, "I don't think nationality matters."

Roma smothered a laugh as McCabe ushered her out of the restaurant.

"I'm beginning to feel like an object," he murmured. "What were you trying to do, sell me?"

"They were ready to buy." She tilted her head back and looked at him as they walked, caught between delight at being able to tease him and the constricting inner tension that just being near him caused. "How much are you worth?"

A lightning grin flashed across his face, unsettling her even more. "More than they can afford."

They strolled toward the entrance to the casino, encased in a silence that prickled with awareness and yet was oddly intimate. His hand was warm and heavy at her back, increasing her awareness of the man at her side until her senses were so acutely attuned to that point of contact that the slightest shift of his fingers sent sharp little bursts of sensation through her.

McCabe lifted a hand to one of the security guys. Addie Carson, a permanent resident of the hotel whom Roma had met a couple of times, spotted them and stopped to say hello. A few minutes later, they continued on toward the elevator.

McCabe's hand was still firm at the hollow of her back, his touch natural, courteous, consistent with the need for them to appear close, but there was no audience now, no professional reason for him to touch her.

Seconds later, McCabe relinquished his hold to operate the elevator. Roma's fingers tightened on the strap of her holdall as the lift moved slowly upward, then stopped with a small cushioned jolt, and she finally faced the source of her panic. It was night, and she and McCabe were going about the ritual of returning to their hotel room as if they were a couple.

She felt as skittish as if he were going to jump her any second, which was ridiculous. The attraction cut both ways with her and McCabe, but the fact remained that he was her bodyguard...no matter how much she wished he wasn't.

McCabe unlocked the door and ushered her in. She walked a few steps, spine rigid with the knowledge that he was behind her. He said her name. She half turned, and he almost walked into her. His hand shot around her waist to steady her; his eyes locked hard with hers. A quiver went through her as he lowered his head.

The kiss was short and soft and deliberate, a tester that sent a bolt of heat straight to her loins so that she stood still in his grasp, blinking, barely able to breathe.

The strap of her holdall slipped off her shoulder, and the bag dropped to the floor with a muffled clunk. She hardly noticed.

His hand settled at her nape, warm and heavy as he coaxed her forward until she was standing between his legs. "I've wanted to do that ever since I saw you at the airport."

She had time to draw a quick breath; then his mouth settled on hers, this time firm, pressing her lips apart, his tongue sliding deep.

A moan shivered up from deep in her belly and locked in her throat. Her fingers closed on the lapels of his jacket as the softly lit lounge faded into hazy oblivion. Oh, yes, she wanted this.

The first time McCabe had looked at her she'd received the instant impression that he knew his way around a woman's body just a little too well. Now she knew it. Sexual confidence radiated from him like high-octane gas shimmering off a hot runway. He knew exactly how to touch her, his palm burning the bare skin of her nape, fingers tangled in her hair, lips soft and rough in turn, tongue sliding in a hot sinuous rhythm in her mouth.

He stepped in closer, keeping his mouth hard on hers as he crowded her back against the wall. His muscled thigh slid between hers as he pressed close enough that she felt the hard ridge of his arousal against her hip.

A raw shock of awareness jolted through her. The few times she'd dealt with male arousal, she'd been repelled; it had been her signal to stop, but she didn't feel repelled now. McCabe's arousal filled her with a shivering excitement. She wanted to press closer, to rub against him, and she wondered, dazed, what was happening to her. She'd dated, kissed, necked, dreamed about how it would be, but she'd never lost control.

The kiss turned raw and primitive, his tongue shoving deep, his arm clamped around her waist so that she was arched against him, her breasts flattened against the muscular wall of his chest. Heat exploded through her, and a strangled sob worked its way up from her throat, dying a muffled death against his lips.

He lifted his mouth, shrugged out of his jacket and tossed it aside. When she slipped her arms around his waist, her hand bumped against the hard shape that was his gun encased in its holster. The presence of the weapon reminded her of who McCabe was, what he was, but that information spiralled away when his mouth settled hungrily back on hers.

The wall was hard behind her, deliciously cool, when every part of her was burning up and damp with perspiration. His hands cupped her breasts, his thumbs rubbed across her nipples, and she moaned out loud, her head falling back as the ache between her legs became feverishly hot. He said something low and rough beneath his breath; then his arm tightened around her waist, and one big hand cupped her bottom, massaging the tender, sensitive flesh as he lifted her against him, his thighs pressing hers apart so she could feel the heavy bulge of his arousal pushing between her legs, rubbing against the hot, sharp ache.

She gripped his shoulders as his hand closed around her breast, his hold firm, so that the nipple was achingly erect. He dipped and fastened his mouth on her through the layers of cloth. The strong, drawing sensation made her tense and arch, her heart pounding, all the breath gone from her lungs, so that all she could do was hold on and endure as heat gathered, intensified, threatening to swamp her. He bit down gently, and pleasure burst through her, burned between her legs where the blunt ridge of his sex was firmly lodged, the pressure insistent, as if he could penetrate her through the barrier of their clothes.

His head lifted, his blue eyes glittering, the heat and power of him overwhelming as he held her pinned against the wall. "I want you."

The words were low and strained, as if they'd been forced from him. His gaze burned into her as he waited. Roma lifted lids that felt heavy, weighted. She knew what McCabe wanted, knew that this was happening fast—way too fast—but she didn't want to resist. She was a healthy female animal, and she'd spent years being sensible, years wondering what drove intelligent women to make incomprehensible decisions about men, to merrily toss their careers and sometimes their freedom away. Now she knew. She could barely think, barely function, beyond enduring the storm of sensation that battered her. Her clothes were twisted and too tight, clinging uncomfortably to her skin; her breasts were throbbing and sensitive, so that she wanted to rub against McCabe's hard, muscled chest to ease the ache.

Her arms wound around his neck. "Yes," she said simply.

A rough sound was torn from his throat. His mouth sank down hard on hers, and she whimpered with relief, her stomach jumping nervously at the decision she'd just made.

She felt the waistband of her pants loosen, the rough bunching as they were pushed down her hips, the startling glide of his fingers sliding beneath her panties. Then he was cupping her, his palm hot, the pads of his fingers rough. She had a moment to grasp the crude intimacy of his bare hand against her naked, sensitive flesh, the stunning speed with which he had moved; then she felt him parting her folds and a finger pushed shallowly inside her.

At the first shock of the intrusion she began to climax, clinging to his shoulders as he withdrew and pushed inside her again. This time the thickness of the invasion made her stiffen, and she realised he'd penetrated her with two fingers, pushing deeper than before so that she was stretched tight around him, burning and throbbing.

McCabe said something low and soft beneath his breath, and went very still against her. His chest rose and fell sharply; she could feel the rapid slam of his heart. His fingers were still lodged inside her, alien and uncomfortable, the throbbing ache existing somewhere on the uneasy border between pleasure and pain, so that part of her wanted to shrink back from the pressure and the stretching, and another part of her wanted to press against him and recklessly invite him deeper.

"You're a virgin." A moment of utter silence followed his statement. He sighed, his breath stirring her hair. His forehead dropped down on hers as his fingers slowly withdrew, leaving an aching dampness behind. "I'm glad I found out before I went any further."

A little chill went through her at the mildness of McCabe's tone. She knew he was aroused, knew that seconds ago he'd been wild for her, but the swiftness with which he'd regained his control was like a slap in the face. Apart from the obvious physical sign of his arousal, he could have been reciting a grocery list.

He pushed away from her, bent and retrieved his jacket. Suddenly awkward, Roma jerked her pants up and fastened them, yanking on the zip, her jaw clamping when the teeth snagged.

"Need some help?"

She tugged at the zip. "I've been dressing myself since I was four. I think I can manage."

She finally worked the zip up, her face flushing with heat as she straightened her top, which had twisted around her waist. McCabe had had her pinned against that wall while he'd done things to her, turning her bones to jelly and shattering her view of life in general, and sex in particular. Now she knew what the fuss was all about, and she felt like crying. She was achey and tender, her whole body throbbing, her legs so limp it was a wonder she could stand. After all these years of not feeling anything memorable, McCabe had reduced her to a trembling mass of nerve endings barely capable of thought.

It hadn't taken much. All he'd had to do was push her up against a wall and she'd climaxed. *They hadn't even made love.*

Bending, she snagged the strap of her holdall and

hooked it over her shoulder. Her gun bumped against her hip, reminding her that she'd been careless enough to drop it and now she needed to check that it was still safe.

"Why?" McCabe demanded softly.

Roma's head came up at the cool demand.

McCabe was watching her, his expression back to unfathomable, the lines of cheekbone and jaw sharply delineated by the lamplight. With his muscular arms bare and the black utilitarian lines of the shoulder holster visible, he looked tough and controlled. Apart from the bulge in his pants it was hard to believe he'd been aroused at all.

"Were you saving yourself for Mr. Right?"

If his tone had been mocking, she wouldn't have answered. "Not especially. I just haven't been bothered."

"Haven't been bothered?" McCabe gazed at her, arrested.

Roma began to wonder if she'd grown an extra head. "What's so strange about that? Not everyone becomes sexually active the second they hit puberty."

"You're twenty-four. Most people have an interest before then."

She eyed him coolly. "Did I say I wasn't interested?"

"Okay, then…why me, and why now?"

Before she could answer, he shook his head. "No. Forget I asked that. It's late, and we could both do with a good night's sleep.'' He turned away, shrugging out of the shoulder rig.

Her jaw squared at the dismissal. "And that's it?"

He stopped, holster dangling from his fingers, his broad back still, and she was suddenly aware that McCabe wasn't as cold and unmoved as he looked. Her stomach clenched on a jab of apprehension, and she wondered what had happened to her judgement. Goading McCabe was a bit like prodding a big battle-scarred tiger with a stick.

"Don't push it," he said softly, half turning. "You're a virgin. In my book that changes the rules."

In her book, if you loved someone, that had been the rule. She didn't love McCabe, but on some primitive level everything inside her had shouted loud and clear that it had been right with him. "I never would have picked you for a traditionalist."

"When it comes to your family, I damn well better be."

Chapter 10

Roma sat up in bed and fumbled for the light switch, blinking as the room flooded with golden light. Shoving tangled hair back from her face, she took a calming breath. It was one in the morning, and hot. She'd been tossing and turning for hours, and the thin cotton tank top she wore clung damply to her skin. She'd slept the day away, and now she was wide awake, her mind running over and over what had happened between her and McCabe, and every now and then, just for a change of pace, sliding sideways into the shooting.

Pushing the covers back, she climbed from the bed, walked to the window and held the curtain back. The night was clear, the stars visible, although faint—their glitter diminished by the radiant glow of the city.

With an impatient movement, she pushed the window wide, leaned her arms on the sill and breathed in the cool softness of the night air as she searched out the elusive patterns in the night sky. The flesh of her arms rose in response to the cooler air, the faint chill sliding through her, bringing with it a wave of loneliness that seemed to sink into her very bones. Standing in the still silence of her room, she felt isolated and alone in a way she'd never experienced before.

It had to do with McCabe. He'd backed off so fast it hurt. She recognised that rigid code of honour, had seen it operating in her brothers. She'd joked with them about it often enough when they were single. It was almost as if they had some kind of internal radar, and if they decided a woman was a virgin, she got to stay that way, regardless of what she wanted. McCabe probably thought he was doing her a favour, and maybe he was, but all the same, she couldn't help wondering what it would have been like.

The dull throbbing low in her belly sharpened, her nipples tightening until they were almost painfully tender, and so sensitive she could hardly bear the clinging softness of her tank top. She blew out a disgusted breath. She was frustrated. In male terms, horny. This wasn't supposed to happen. Every little girl struggling with puberty got to learn that when it came to sex, men were at best easy, at worst like wild animals on the prowl. In theory she should have to guard herself against McCabe.

With a sigh, she pushed away from the window and paced the length of the room. She should have a shower to help her sleep, but if she did that she would probably wake McCabe, and that was the last thing she wanted; she'd already had her full measure of humiliation for one night.

As much as she despised the sleeping pills, she wished she had one now.

Grimly, she got down on the carpet and began to do smooth sets of exercises, focusing her mind on the repetitive movements and *not* McCabe, working her muscles until sweat sheened her skin. If she was physically tired she had a better chance of sleeping—real sleep, minus the dreams.

Half an hour later she changed into fresh panties and a tank top, climbed back into bed and finally fell headlong into sleep.

A sound jerked Ben awake. He rolled off the bed, naked but for a pair of stretchy grey boxers, reached for the Glock and slicked the clip into place as he moved across the room.

The sound had been low, muffled; he couldn't identify exactly what it was—the slide of a footstep, a soft groan.

He eased the drapes aside and checked the terrace. Moonlight flooded most of the area with bright silver light, plunged other parts into inky blackness. It was empty of movement except for the potted palms shivering in the faint breeze.

He left the curtains open to partially illuminate his room and ghosted into the bathroom, keeping to the shadows. Briefly, he listened at Roma's door, then silently entered her room. She was in bed, asleep, lying utterly still. He listened a moment longer, then left.

He checked the rest of the suite and tested all the locks. When he was satisfied that nothing was amiss, he flicked on a lamp, sat down at his desk and checked the surveillance cameras, then called up tapes of the last ten minutes, studying each as it played through. He didn't expect to find anything, and he didn't. The Lombard suite was isolated from every other in the hotel and had its own private lift. If anyone came up here they would have to obtain a key and the PIN number that went with it, and then they would be under constant, overt surveillance all the way. The defences had been breached—once—but since then, the Lombard family had upped the security. When they were in residence now, they had twenty-four-hour live surveillance on the lift and the short corridor leading to the suite.

He closed the programme and strolled back to his room, placed the Glock on the bedside table, unlocked the terrace doors and walked outside. The terracotta tiles were cool beneath his bare feet, and beaded with condensation. He padded to the iron railing and stared out over the glittering cityscape and the gleaming expanse of sea, nostrils flaring as he drank in the warm, damp air, the faint bite of salt.

The wind had shifted to the northeast and now wheeled in off the ocean, bringing with it a hot, wet front, fresh from the tropics, which explained why it was hot as a bitch. It was going to rain.

Seconds later, as if to prove his point, the leading edge of a heavy bank of clouds slid across the face of the moon, cutting off the stark flood of silver light. The abrupt transition from light to darkness intensified the illusion that the whole city was being slowly smothered beneath a blanket of humidity.

A low rumble of thunder sounded. Out at sea, lightning flared across the roughening surface of the water. The breeze picked up, feathering through the palms and fanning his sweat-dampened skin, although it was more a warm stirring of the atmosphere than a true breeze, and didn't provide any relief.

Ben went back inside, leaving the doors open, and lay down on top of his rumpled bed. He was tempted to sleep naked, because he was still aroused from what had happened earlier that night, his skin so ultra-sensitive he could barely stand even the soft gloving of interlock, but that wasn't an option when he was working. There were enough things that could go wrong without getting caught with his pants down.

Thunder grumbled again, closer this time, the low register of sound putting him even more on edge so that he stared at the ceiling with slitted eyes, not inclined to sleep. What he wanted was to walk into Roma's room, strip the bedclothes from her and finish what they'd started against that wall, virgin or not.

The thought made his heart pound and sweat slick his skin. He'd never felt like this, so hungry he was bordering on desperate. If he didn't have his daughter to consider, the mistake of his last marriage burned into his brain, he would be in bed with Roma now, instead of holding on to honour as an excuse.

She'd called him on it, and he hadn't lied. He didn't want to do anything to hurt either her or her family, but at one o'clock in the morning, his body tight with frustration, he was beginning to question his logic. Roma was twenty-four, and independent. If she wanted to go to bed for the first time with a man, she would, regardless of whether her family approved or not.

The thought of her lying naked beneath another man made his hands tighten into fists. He was beginning to think he'd been crazy turning her down. Crazy, and commitment shy.

Minutes ticked by. The thunder continued to rumble, the vibration low-key, sporadic. Shafts of hot, intense light seared through the gloom as lightning periodically lit up the sky, but the rain held off, and the sultry heat built until the air was heavy and charged with ozone.

Abruptly, the breeze strengthened, whipping the gauzy curtains and sending the first scattering of rain into the room. Ben got up to close the doors just as the heavens opened and rain came down in a torrent.

Damp muslin plastered against his thighs, the rain soaking him in seconds as he fastened the doors. Grimly, he shoved a hand through his hair, slicking the moisture back so that it ran in a tepid rivulet down his spine as he walked into the bathroom for a towel. His gaze fixed broodingly on the door that opened into Roma's room as he jerked his towel off the rail and began drying his hair.

It was going to be a long night.

The sound catapulted him from sleep. It was louder this time, a low howl that sent cold spearing down his spine, making all the hairs at his nape stand on end.

He reached Roma's room, the Glock in his hand, and swung the door wide. It banged softly against the wall. The howl came again, low and rending, like an animal in pain, and he froze, then let his arms drop, the Glock held loose in his fingers.

Roma hadn't pulled the curtains, and the ambient light produced by the inner city cast a dim glow into the room, enough for him to see that she was asleep, despite the noise she'd made. He laid the gun down on the bedside table and flicked on the lamp. Something twisted inside him. She was crying in her sleep.

Roma surfaced at the first touch, immediately aware that McCabe was bending over her, his hand gripping her shoulder. She was also aware that at some time during the night she'd kicked the covers off and now her skin was damp and clammy, and she was shuddering as if she were in the grip of a fever.

He made her sit up, grabbed the feather-soft blanket that was draped at the end of the bed and wrapped it around her, brushing aside her apology for waking him.

The mattress sank as he sat down beside her and picked up her wrist. The clasp of his hand sent a tingling jolt up her arm.

His gaze pinned her as he measured her pulse. "Do you need me to call a doctor?"

She took a steadying breath, caught somewhere between embarrassment and resignation, and relieved when he released her wrist. This was the third time McCabe had surprised her while she was asleep. She felt like saying, "We've got to stop meeting like this," but instead repeated what she'd said earlier. "I'm sorry I woke you. It was just a dream…a bad dream I have sometimes."

Only this one had been worse than usual. Much worse.

Instead of getting up and leaving, as she'd expected, he remained where he was. "Care to tell me about it?"

His invitation surprised the words out of her. "I dream about Jake."

Her statement hung starkly in the silence of the room, and she wondered how she could have told him something so intimate, when she hadn't talked about the dreams with any member of her family.

But maybe that was it. McCabe wasn't family, and there was a sense of relief in finally telling someone. The dream had been with her for years, drifting through her nights, sometimes surfacing in daydreams. It had haunted her, but now that she'd given it its first tentative airing, it didn't seem nearly so painful or mysterious.

She loosened the soft folds of the blanket as the warmth became uncomfortable, letting it slide from her shoulders to puddle around her waist. "They never found his body." Even now flinching from saying that dehumanizing word "body". "Rafaella washed up, but not Jake." She rubbed her fingers over her forehead, pushed tangled hair back from her face. "I keep dreaming that he's alive."

Ben's chest tightened on an intake of air. He'd never met Jake, but he'd seen photos of him. He was a year or so older than Gray, big and vital, larger than life in every way. Over the years, with the hunt for Jake's killer, the oldest Lombard brother had loomed large in Ben's life, despite the fact that he was dead and gone. Even now, it was hard to imagine all that bright burning power snuffed out. "You haven't talked to your family about the dream?"

Her head came up sharply. "They don't need to know."

The hell they didn't, he thought grimly. She'd been shaking, crying in her sleep. Her whole system had gone into shock.

The shooting three nights ago had obviously triggered the old trauma. He'd seen that happen after combat situations, especially if there'd been a death. Guys would put on a good face, seem to shrug it off. The next thing, they were in the psych unit undergoing evaluation.

All the stories he'd heard about Roma suddenly clicked into place in his mind. She'd been a teenager when Jake had been killed, little more than a child, and she'd let off steam in her own way—a way that had made her family laugh when they hadn't had a lot to laugh about. As she'd moved into adulthood the wild antics had stopped and she'd closed off, pulling into herself and repressing the fears, which was a natural enough process, but now he was worried about her. She hadn't cried or complained or asked for comfort while she was awake. Her vulnerability had only surfaced during sleep, wrenched out of her with that unearthly howl.

If he tried to question her, she would treat him to more of the same blank routine. He would have to find out in more subtle ways. He didn't want to scare her or make her any more wary of him than she already was. He wanted her to trust him, to let down her barriers.

He went still inside, aware of the decision he'd just made. Nothing was settled between them, but right or wrong, the next time Roma dreamed about Jake, she wouldn't be alone.

She fished the blanket out from around herself and let it drop onto the floor, then hugged her knees to her chest. "You can go back to bed. I'm all right now."

"No, you're not." He kept his expression neutral, his voice calm, so as not to alarm her. He needed to be gentle now, to soothe her enough that she would relax with him. "If it helps, we may never have found Jake, but I was part of the team that hunted Harper down. I saw his body. He's dead. I know that doesn't bring your brother back, but Harper and the entire terrorist cell he ran are gone. There was only one guy we couldn't account for, and we didn't expect to find him, because he was a contract hit man and had no known affiliations with any terrorist group. Gray still has feelers out, looking for him, but he doesn't hold out much hope. Those guys work strictly for hire, and they're close to invisible."

A chill walked down Roma's spine at the matter-of-fact recital. She kept forgetting how close McCabe was to her brothers. In some ways he was so tied to her family, he might as well *be* family.

"Get under the covers. I'll get you something to drink."

He stood, making her aware that he was naked except for a pair of stretchy boxers that clung to his thighs and hugged his muscular butt. As he strode from the room, golden lamplight slid over his broad, tanned back, shadowing the deep indentation of his spine

When he disappeared from sight, she let out a breath and slipped beneath the covers. She was still dazed by what had happened, the emotional upheaval of the dream and the unexpected gentleness of McCabe's response when she'd braced herself for another rejection.

Sleepily, she wondered what it would feel like to have him in bed with her. He was big and sleekly muscled. He would be heavy, and hot. A little shudder ran through her, and her stomach contracted around a painful throb of desire. She already knew just how hot. She'd already experienced the heat that poured from him, the disconcerting electrical tingle. She wanted that, still wanted *him,* despite what had happened before she'd gone to bed.

A short time later he returned with a glass of milk, then sat down beside her on the bed, quietly watching while she drank. She got the impression that if he hadn't thought she was capable of holding the glass, he would have held it for her. When she was finished, she handed him the empty glass and he set it down on the bedside table. Instead of leaving, he peeled the sheet back and slid in beside her.

The lamp was flicked off, plunging the room into darkness. His arm curled around her waist, pulling her close. The weight of his arm, the intense heat of his body, shocked her into immobility so that she lay rigid. "What are you doing?"

"Sleeping with you," he murmured beside her ear. "Relax, I won't bite unless you want me to."

Chapter 11

The thunder woke her, low and sullen, vibrating through the darkness and making the night seem even more oppressive, as if the churning power of the storm had sucked up all the oxygen in its path.

For a hazy moment she wondered why she was so hot, her skin dewed with perspiration, when she was practically naked, with no bed coverings on her. Then she came fully awake. She was lying half on top of McCabe, one leg tangled between his, her head nestled on his shoulder, one arm flung across his chest.

The steady pounding of his heart thudded in her ear. She could feel the hard power of his thigh beneath her leg, the searing heat of his hand where it rested on the bare skin at the small of her back.

She rose up and stared down into McCabe's face, aware by the subtle tension in his body, the rhythm of his breathing, that he was awake. Lightning flickered, filling the room with a silvery radiance and glittering in McCabe's half-closed eyes. The hot weight of his hand shifted, glided upward, taking her tank top with it, so that her belly rubbed against his. He pulled the limp cotton from her arms and over her head, his hands returning to cup her naked breasts, his palms hot and rough against her much cooler skin, thumbs rasping across her nipples so that they sprang swollen and erect.

His thigh shifted, riding up between her legs until hard muscle rubbed against the sensitive, tender folds of her sex, and a moan stirred from deep in her throat. Even with her panties on, the sensation was close to unbearable. The pressure of his thigh was replaced with his hand as he stroked between her legs, rubbing through the damp cling of cotton, his voice low and soothing as she twisted against him.

He coaxed her up his body until she was straddling him, supporting herself on her hands; then he lifted his head to suckle her, his movements slow and deliberate, almost lazy, the wet pull of his mouth strong, the drawing sensation sharp in the dreamlike well of the night.

Rain spattered against glass, the drops slow and ponderous, marking out the slow, restless passage of time as she was caught and held by the rough heat of McCabe's hands, his mouth, the pleasure that jerked through her in waves.

Abruptly, his hands closed on her waist and she found herself lying on her back, his solid weight pressing her into the mattress as he settled between her thighs. The hard jut of his sex prodded her soft folds through the barrier of their clothes, shoved at her entrance.

"If you want me to stop, say so now," he said in a low voice.

For answer, Roma pulled his head down to hers. He groaned as she kissed him, and a shudder moved through his body, filling her with a sense of amazement at just how much she could affect him.

McCabe lifted himself a bare few inches from her, stripped her panties off and shoved his boxers down, then reached for something on the bedside table. She heard the rustle of foil as she pulled his mouth back to hers. The weight of his body settled on her, and she felt the blunt satiny shape of him prodding between her folds, the pleasure so exquisite she bucked against him.

Abruptly, the broad head of his sex lodged in her entrance. There was a moment of utter stillness, then McCabe shuddered, groaned against her lips and plunged inside her, the intrusion so thick that she froze, her whole body stiffening at the immensity of the thrust, the shock of penetration.

With a muffled curse McCabe pulled free, rearing back on the bed.

She had a moment of stunned realisation as she saw the swollen jut of his sex, saw him rip a foil packet open and smooth a condom down the length of the shaft.

His shoulders were broad as he loomed over her, the muscular lines of his body as powerful and sleek as a big cat's as he reached between them and fitted himself to her entrance. "I'm sorry if that hurt," he said low and rough. "I promise I'll make it as easy as I can."

She tensed at the burning pressure, the sense of impalement, as he pressed inward and abruptly breached that first tight constriction. He stopped, chest heaving, gaze locked with hers; then with one heavy shove he was inside her.

They stayed like that for endless minutes as she struggled to adjust to the muscular thickness of him forging deep in her belly. She felt smothered and hot, her skin welded slickly to his wherever they touched, but the shattering intimacy of what McCabe was doing to her held her.

Rain pounded on the window in solid sheets, but the breaking storm didn't bring any relief; the atmosphere was moisture-laden and murky, settling like a damp shroud so that every breath was an effort. Lightning flickered through the room, outlining McCabe's shoulders, gleaming with sweat, the stark line of his cheekbone, the barbaric lash of the scar. Her gaze fastened on his, and a tingling chill quivered along the length of her spine. His eyes were glittering hot, utterly aware, as he reached between them and rubbed the swollen, taut flesh just above where he penetrated her. He stroked once, twice, his fingertips dragging over the acutely sensitive bud, and she arched at the hot shock of her climax, crying out wildly.

He began to move as she lay beneath him, limp and dazed by the power of her climax. She heard his voice, low and rough, cajoling, and realised he wanted her to wind her legs around his waist.

The different angle relieved some of the rasping pressure, and he was moving more easily now. He dipped and took her breast in his mouth, and the hot, stirring pleasure gripped her again, pushing her over some invisible edge so that she moaned and lifted her hips to meet the plunge of his, her fingers tangling in his hair, gripping him tight, as he moved to her other breast.

The tension coiled and built on endless waves of heat until she was dazed, all the breath pushed from her lungs. He bit down gently, and her climax hit her again. He shoved deep in that same moment. Her whole body quivered at the shock, her legs slipping limply from his waist. One big hand gripped her buttocks, held her locked hard against him as he shuddered against her. She felt the muscular pulsing spasms start deep in her belly, had a moment of startled recall. McCabe had stopped to pull on a condom, so he wasn't naked inside her. There was no chance of pregnancy, because that intimate part of him was sheathed in latex and wasn't actually touching her; then there was only the steady drumbeat of the rain, the dizzying, suffocating darkness, and the burning awareness of McCabe still on top of her, the alien, throbbing pressure where he still penetrated her.

McCabe watched Roma as she slept. He should ease himself out, get some sleep himself, but he wasn't going to. He knew that if he withdrew for any length of time, he wouldn't be able to penetrate her again tonight, and he was still hungry, still heavily aroused. He was going to stay on top of her and inside her as long as he could.

She had been a virgin. His jaw tightened.

And he'd damn near made her pregnant. The magnitude of the mistake he'd almost made alarmed him. He'd lost control. He'd had the condom in his hand, but he hadn't wanted to use it. He'd wanted to be naked inside her, and when she'd shoved against him, he'd given in to temptation and had slid inside her. The pleasure had been so acute, he'd almost lost it completely.

It was male and primitive, dumb-ass stupid, but he still wanted to slide into her naked, still wanted to pump his sperm into her until he made her pregnant. He guessed that was what made the world go around. Getting Nicola pregnant had certainly changed his world once, although that had been a genuine mistake, *his mistake*—trusting to a contraceptive pill. Since then, he'd always travelled with a supply of condoms, and he would never have imagined that he would consciously tempt fate by having unprotected sex. He'd worked too hard, hurt too hard, to let his life be pushed off course by the whim of sexual need.

Grimly, he withdrew, dispensed with the used condom, sheathed himself again and gently slid back, smooth and deep. Her muscles gradually relaxed around him, and he began to move, unable to remain passive until she woke. He felt fierce, possessive, and completely unsettled by the need that burned through him. He was grasping for a measure of control, and for the first time in his adult life, control was eluding him.

She must have slept. Roma woke, drowsy and exhausted, to find McCabe moving over her. She was vaguely aware that he'd remained inside her as she'd slept, that he'd only removed himself to sheath himself, to pull on another condom, then he'd slid into her again. This time the glide of penetration was smoother. The climax sneaked up on her, slow and hot and endless, shimmering through her until she grew disoriented, unsure if she was awake or dreaming.

It was still raining as she drifted in that curious limbo. The steady drumming muffled the sounds of the city, created a drugging sense of intimacy, so that she had the oddest sense of being cut off from the rest of the world, isolated and enclosed in stifling shadows, too tired to move.

McCabe lay sprawled between her legs and off to the side, dozing, but still lodged firmly inside her. The dense heat of his big body blasted her, and wherever they touched, her skin was flushed with heat and slick with perspiration. Sleepily, she examined the quivering leap of excitement in her tummy every time she consciously registered the raw animal intimacy of having McCabe on top of her, inside her.

The initial pain seemed hazy and distant now, obliterated by the hot, endless wash of pleasure. She was fuzzy on how many times they'd made love. Maybe it had been more than twice. She decided she was actually getting used to having McCabe inside her, despite the fact that the first time had hurt.

She drew one leg up to ease her back. Her inner thigh rasped against the powerful line of McCabe's thigh. Experimentally, she contracted the muscles between her legs, clasping him more tightly. The warm, tingling throb sharpened, spread, so that her nipples tightened. She felt McCabe stir and thicken in response, his sex prodding deeper.

His hand glided up from her belly to her breast, a sleepy, lazy touch that made her want to stretch and rub herself against him like a contented cat. Dimly she became aware that he'd propped himself on one elbow and was watching her as he played with her breast, his eyes a narrow glitter in the darkness. He caught one nipple between his thumb and forefinger, making the throb between her legs more insistent.

Her breath came in sharply, and she voiced the

thought that hovered at the edge of her conscious-
ness. "What made you change your mind?"

Her eyes flickered wide at the unfamiliar sound of
her own voice, husky and faintly slurred, as if she
was drugged by the sweltering heat of the night, held
in thrall to the man lying over her. Abruptly, the
strangeness of what was happening swept her.

"I couldn't stand not having you."

The words were low, matter-of-fact, like a dash of
cold water in the thick heat of the room, intensifying
the disorienting strangeness of lying naked beneath
a man she'd met less than twenty-four hours ago.

He shifted more firmly over her, dipped and took
her nipple into his mouth. The wet rasp of his tongue
made her arch helplessly, and the moment of disori-
entation spun away. Her fingers sank into his hair,
holding him against her, as he continued to suckle
her breasts. This time he didn't move between her
legs, simply held himself deep, anchoring her solidly
beneath him while she shivered and arched, desperate
for the aching hot glide of his sex, and enduring the
spasm of pleasure every time he used the edge of his
teeth.

The tension low in her belly grew sharper, so that
she clenched and throbbed around him, lifting her
hips in mute frustration while he played with her
breasts, until in desperation she grabbed his head and
pulled his mouth to hers. He muttered something savage. His hips jackhammered as he shoved deep, and
heat burst through her in dizzying waves.

* * *

She awoke several times to find McCabe sliding in and out of her, but her memory was vague, muddled, as if the thrusting had been prolonged and had stretched over a long period of time. McCabe had kept her spread and beneath him the whole time. She felt stretched and achey in an unfamiliar way, her body leaden with exhaustion, yet she was curiously contented. The night had changed her in a basic way, so that she'd become utterly used to McCabe's touch, his weight and the male scent of him, the peculiarly animal comfort of continued penetration.

The next time she woke, the room was bright with sunlight.

"All right?" McCabe asked in a low, dark murmur.

He was sprawled next to her, propped on his side, one hand curved, warm and heavy, around her breast. Sometime in the night he'd pulled the sheet over them both, so that it draped his hips, leaving his torso bare. The broad, muscled expanse of his chest, with its dark sprinkling of hair, was subtly shocking in the light of day, bringing home the raw physicality of the night. She felt stiff and sore all over, her muscles aching in odd places. "Sore."

"I'll get you something for that. You're going to need it."

His hand slid down over her belly, between her legs. She flinched. She felt tender and swollen, but she opened for him as he pushed the sheet away and

let him gently examine her, so used to him touching
her intimately, she didn't even think of protesting.
Despite her soreness, the glide of his fingers made
her shiver inside and her breasts tighten in anticipation.

His head lifted, and his gaze narrowed on hers.
His hand was still between her legs, cupping her pos-
sessively. She felt the gliding stroke of his finger as
he slowly penetrated, and her eyes closed, her breath
catching in her throat.

When her lashes lifted, he was watching her with
a heavy-lidded intensity she'd come to recognise.
The sheet had fallen away from his hips, so that his
genitals were plainly visible, and her eyes widened
at his size. His arousal jutted bluntly from between
powerful thighs, the shaft thick and heavy. It was no
wonder she was sore. She'd seen male genitalia in
magazines and books, a couple of foreign films, but
she'd never actually seen a fully erect male up close,
and last night she'd only caught glimpses in the dark.
Her heart pounded as he leaned down and kissed her,
his tongue delving with a leisurely familiarity as he
continued to stroke between her legs, inserting a second finger so that she tensed at the fullness of penetration, a muffled moan drifting from her throat.

He pressed gently with his thumb just above her
opening, so that she arched and clung to his shoulders as she clenched helplessly around him.

When he lifted his head, his eyes burned a hot

blue. "I'll go shopping for lubricant this morning. I'm not waiting days to have you again."

Before she could answer, a buzzing sound took McCabe's attention.

He glanced at the bedside clock. "That'll be Bunny."

Easing his fingers from her, he flipped the sheet back and strolled, naked, from the room, calmly ignoring his arousal, all his attention abruptly focused on his daughter.

Roma heard the murmur of his voice as he picked up the call in his room, then, a few minutes later, laughter. She lay, still and silent, her body heavy, head vaguely swimmy with exhaustion, still throbbing and tingling from his touch.

He didn't stroll back into the room with the phone, as she expected, but stayed talking in his own room. As the minutes ticked by, her skin cooled so that she drew the sheet up to cover herself.

Her eyelids drooped. After a few seconds she drifted into a light doze, but despite her tiredness, she couldn't sleep. She felt restless, unsettled, and…shut out.

Her eyes flickered open, and she frowned. After the hours they'd spent locked together, she'd assumed McCabe wanted closeness. Unconsciously, she'd been waiting for him not only to stroll in with the phone, but to get back into bed and cuddle her while he finished the call. Before the phone had rung, he'd been completely absorbed in her—if she hadn't been so chafed, he would have been making love to her.

A chill prickled at her nape, spread until it settled coldly in her stomach. She stared blindly at the lazy rotation of the ceiling fan. But then maybe he didn't want closeness? How would she know what McCabe wanted? They'd barely spoken except to argue. McCabe had held her the day before when he'd been worried about the effects of the sleeping pill, he'd comforted her last night before he'd gotten into bed with her, but apart from that he hadn't cuddled her. When she'd woken, he'd stripped and penetrated her within minutes. His lovemaking had been fierce and prolonged, and he'd taken care that she'd climaxed often, but all his touching had been sexual.

She hadn't known until that moment what exactly had been missing, or how much she wanted softness from McCabe, but now she couldn't ignore the lack, because it was monumental. They'd met and gone to bed within a matter of hours; there hadn't been time to form a relationship, and, as earth-shattering as the lovemaking had been, it was the relationship that was important to Roma.

She wanted all the things that most women wanted: to hold hands and cuddle, be petted and spoiled and indulged, taken out to dinner and treated like a princess. She didn't need expensive presents or jewellery. What she needed was to be loved.

She'd taken one look at McCabe and been pole-axed; she was happy to admit that, because it was nothing less than the truth. She'd let her emotions rule her head. Then she'd made the basic mistake of equating sex with love.

But McCabe hadn't.

When the telephone had rung, he had neatly separated her from his personal life, his child; the dismissive way he'd shut her out as neat as flicking a switch.

Yesterday he'd made it clear he didn't want to discuss Bunny with her in the truck. Now he was carefully keeping his child separate from her. She couldn't blame him. He had his responsibility as a parent to consider, and his small daughter had to rank before her in his life.

And why would he allow her any entrée into his very private family life if he had no intention of her ever being a part of it?

She was naive. A fool. Just because McCabe was her first lover, she'd automatically assumed they would have some kind of relationship, when, if she was brutally honest, all they'd shared was sex. Mind-blowing, drugging, all-night sex.

He'd said he wanted her again.

No. He wanted to *have* her again. There was a difference. He didn't want to make love, he wanted sex—a raw slaking of his appetite.

She remembered waking up in the night to find him sliding in and out of her, too dazed and sleepy to do more than respond blindly. She'd lost count of the times he'd made her climax, once she'd *woken up* climaxing. She had no idea of the number of times they'd made love.

But if she'd lost her head, McCabe hadn't; he had been utterly aware. Apart from the first time he'd penetrated her, he'd been careful to sheath himself with a condom and protect them both from the tie of an unwanted pregnancy.

Her stomach tightened. McCabe must have brought a supply of condoms—not one, but a *supply*—with him when he'd brought her drink in. He had known he was going to have sex with her, and he'd prepared. Even though she knew condoms were a necessary part of any single person's love life, they added a cold layer of calculation to lovemaking.

She swallowed, feeling nauseous. They had only known each other twenty-four hours.

Twenty-four hours.

Her mind groped with the unreality of everything that had happened since she'd first laid eyes on McCabe. He was a stranger she was powerfully attracted to, a stranger whom she'd had something of a crush on, even before they'd met. She'd been tipped off balance by the sheer unexpectedness of the first meeting, then by his cool manner. And now she'd just spent the night with him.

She stared fixedly at the ceiling, heart pounding. She wasn't in love with McCabe. Not after just a few hours.

Nausea welled, pushing at her throat. Shoving the rumpled sheet aside, she swung her legs over the side of the bed and started toward the bathroom. The sudden movement made her head spin, so that she wavered and clutched at the edge of the dresser. Her vision narrowed, dimmed, making her feel even sicker. Drawing a deep breath, she shuffled backward until the backs of her legs hit the bed, sat down hard and shoved her head between her knees. When the blackness receded, she slowly straightened, pushed her hair back from her face and saw herself reflected in the mirror. Her hair was a tangle, her face white, eyes dark in contrast, her mouth swollen.

Gradually her senses filtered back; she could hear the hum of the city waking up, feel the sheet twisted beneath her, smell the heavy, intimate scent of lovemaking that rose from the rumpled cotton. The fan still whispered in the air above her, and a fitful breeze sifted in through the partially open window, adding to the flow of air that feathered her skin, so that she shivered, remembering she was naked.

Taking a deep breath, she looked down at herself, and flinched. Her breasts were reddened and chafed in places from the rasp of McCabe's jaw. There were marks on her hips, her thighs.

She had to cover herself before he came back. Suddenly it seemed very important that he didn't see her naked.

This time, when she stood, she was careful not to move too fast. Her head was still swimmy, but other than that, she was steady as she walked stiffly to the wardrobe, fumbled her silk robe off its hanger and wrapped herself in the familiar, comforting folds.

She could still hear the low hum of McCabe's voice as he talked to his daughter, the pauses when he listened, and everything she didn't know about him hit her like a fist in the stomach, so that she stood, robe hugged around her, too stricken to shuffle the few remaining steps to the bathroom.

She barely knew him. All her information was second-hand, or gleaned over the last day, when she'd been so tired, she'd existed in a haze of exhaustion most of the time.

She knew he loved his daughter, and that he was a close friend of both her brothers. For Blade and Gray to accept McCabe into their ranks meant he had to possess a lot of the same qualities, such as honour, courage, integrity. The very fact that Gray had contracted McCabe to guard her meant he trusted him, and Gray didn't trust easily.

She pressed a shaking hand to her lower belly, feeling the deep tender ache. She had only known McCabe for a matter of hours, and she had let him into her body, without a care for her own protection or pregnancy. Until that moment she had never thought of what it would be like to have a child; that was something for the misty uncertain future, but now reality hit her. If McCabe hadn't provided protection, she could be pregnant now. She should be thankful he'd taken care of it, even if the calculation behind the condoms was upsetting.

She didn't regret making love with McCabe—she'd been wild for him, and after the initial discomfort, she'd loved what he was doing to her, adored the wondrous, almost violent sensations swamping her. She'd loved the feel of him moving inside her, the sheer animal pleasure of his skin against hers, the rub of his body hair, the hot male smell of him. She was stiff and sore from his repeated penetration, but she would have taken him inside her again just minutes ago.

A horrified thought hit her. She closed her eyes briefly. He probably thought she was *easy.*

There was no commitment, no relationship. What they'd had was a steamy one-night stand. As far as she knew, for McCabe, this was just a casual fling.

Chapter 12

Ben terminated the call, strolled naked out into the lounge and deposited his cell phone on the desk, and made a note to call in a couple of extra guys for support. He had broken his own rule by getting sexually involved with a client; therefore, as far as he was concerned, his contract was null and void. His company would do the security at his cost.

Out of habit, he checked the answering machine and listened to the calls, but his mind wasn't on them.

He'd broken more than one rule last night.

Grimly, he considered his position. He wasn't comfortable with what had happened—it had been too fast, too out of control—but he'd made his decision before he'd walked back into Roma's room last night.

He was in relationship territory. Where exactly, he wasn't sure.

The first time he'd laid eyes on Roma, he'd known he had to have her. What he felt was powerfully physical, but if it had been just sex, he could have resisted her. She intrigued and drew him in a way no other woman ever had. Reading the bare facts about how she'd protected Lewis Harrington had sent a cold chill up his spine; not many men would have risked themselves in that way. If she ever tried another stunt like that, he would tan her hide.

The bottom line was that he wanted a relationship. On his terms. But he wasn't sure where the relationship would go, and he wasn't comfortable with his own loss of control.

He didn't trust himself.

That single fact made him incredulous, because he'd never been in this situation, and his fall from grace had happened fast. He needed to slow down, to back off; there was too much at stake in his life to do otherwise.

He didn't want to; he wanted to be with Roma, keep her close. And if he was with her today, he knew he wouldn't be able to resist making love to her. But he wasn't about to let sex force his hand in a relationship ever again. He wanted more, a lot more…and it was going to happen at his pace.

If he spent today with Roma, he would protect her to the letter of the contract, but he couldn't guarantee she wouldn't be pregnant at the end of it.

*   *   *

When Roma walked into the lounge, McCabe was
standing, his back to the open bifold doors, a mug in
his hands. Two men sat sprawled on the sofas, sip-
ping coffee and talking in relaxed tones. She immediately recognised one of the men, Mike Fa'alau,
who was head of security at the hotel. She'd met both
Mike and his father, Tony, who now co-managed the
casino side of the operation with Blade.

Mike got to his feet when he saw her, a slow smile
spreading across his darkly handsome face as Roma
walked up to him and gave him a hug. Mike was tall
and impressively built, with all the reserved power
and grace of his Pacific Island heritage. He was also
happily married, with three gorgeous children. The
entire Fa'alau family was a delight; it encompassed
several generations and overflowed with a powerful,
protective love for anyone within their ranks—including any honorary members, like her own family.

When Mike let her go, McCabe introduced the
young blond man who had risen to his feet.

"Alan works for me. He'll be looking after you
today. When Alan finishes his shift, Charlie Speers
will take his place. You'll meet Charlie later."

Roma stiffened at the cool, professional courtesy
in McCabe's voice, but she was careful to keep her
face blank. "You won't be accompanying me?"

"Not this morning. I've got a few things I need
to attend to."

The phone rang. McCabe strolled to the desk and picked up the call, his back to the room as he spoke.

He was busy. Too busy to personally escort her.

For long seconds Roma couldn't move. She felt frozen, all her muscles locked tight, and then a wave of cold pain prickled through her, breaking the strange stasis. She should have been prepared for this. She had been prepared for this. She didn't have anything high profile happening today, just a fitting session with Evan and some publicity work at the hospital. She didn't need a bodyguard, and she didn't need McCabe, but that wasn't the point.

Roma shook Alan Charter's hand, her movements mechanical. He was medium height and chunkily built, with a crisp military-short haircut, and he was wearing lightweight trousers and loafers, and a dark green collared T-shirt. A gold hoop winked in one ear.

"I know," he said amiably, fingering the earring. "One of these days it's going to get ripped out."

Roma smiled, said something polite in reply, chatted with Mike for the few minutes that McCabe was on the phone, then excused herself and walked blindly out onto the terrace.

The morning breeze tugged at her hair, cut through the lightweight cotton of her cream halter-neck top and pants, as refreshing as a dip in the sea. The sun was hot and strong, burning down onto her bare shoulders. She gulped down a deep breath, then another. She felt numb, stupid, but at least her position was clarified.

She was no longer a virgin, which didn't upset her unduly; the age when women were chattels and their virginity was a commodity to be bartered was long past. The only value she'd ever placed on virginity was a personal one. She felt that it should be given with love, and she *had* given it with love.

She refused to say she'd made a mistake in having sex with McCabe. That hadn't been what she'd wanted out of the encounter, just what she'd ended up with. She had wanted to make love with him, to grab on to something special.

She lifted a hand and smoothed it through her wind-tangled hair, listened to the melancholy cries of the seagulls and grimly faced the death of another illusion. Maybe she'd been living in fairy land, expecting perfection, saving herself for it. In going to bed with McCabe, she'd gotten a dose of reality instead.

The watcher fitted the camera to the tripod, adjusted the zoom. Long brown fingers cupped the lens, stroked the shutter release, sending the motor-driven mechanism into short, rapid-fire bursts. When the roll was finished, he ejected the used film and loaded another with the slick, silent precision of a sniper.

The young woman on the terrace was alone, finally. The big bastard guarding her was efficient. He didn't allow her much space.

"C'mon baby," he crooned. "Turn. Let me see your face."

He waited, comfortable in his stillness, ignoring all the aches and pains that drifted up on him as he stood behind the expanse of smoked glass, the pinching in his spine from the bullet he'd taken while on recon in Borneo in '65, the shrapnel ache in his thigh, courtesy of the Viet Cong in '68.

A lot of people had tried to kill him over the years. Too bad none of them had had enough talent. A bare whisper of humour moved through him at the thought, the humour quickly superseded by a tingling sensation in his head. The tingling increased in intensity until it was a dull burn, momentarily distracting him. When he reacquired his target, the focus was blurred. He frowned as he adjusted the lens, then went still when he realised that the problem wasn't with the focus.

A prickle of alarm went through him. This was something new, and he didn't like it. The one perfect faculty he still possessed was his sight. He couldn't afford to lose it now.

He blinked rapidly. Abruptly, his vision cleared.

The blurring could be a side effect of the experimental drug he was taking—he would check with his source and maybe adjust his dosage down. That was one of the risks with self-medicating, but he was cool with that. The way he figured it, he couldn't do much worse than the damn quacks who'd tried to turn him into a vegetable just months ago.

Of course, the burning tingle and the blurring could be happening for a more ominous reason, but damned if he would dwell on that.

Roma Lombard turned, lifted her dark head to the wind and stared across the deep abyss separating his building from hers—straight into his camera. The eye contact was eerily direct. The illusion that she was standing close enough to touch sent a small shock up his spine, so that all the hairs on the back of his neck lifted and he got hard.

"Oh, yeah," he breathed, "that's it."

Her face blew him away every time. The first time he'd caught that pretty face in his binoculars, his sniper's emotional distance had been ripped away. He'd held the power of life and death in his hands, and he hadn't been able to take her; he'd chosen other members of her family instead.

That decision had done something to him.

Always before, the kill had been close to academic. He'd never allowed himself to become personally involved. He'd planned meticulously, and he'd always worked his plan. One bullet, one moment, then turn away, clean the site, pack his gear and walk—job over.

His inability to consider Roma Lombard a target had driven him crazy, and his mind had dwelled on it the way a tongue prodded a sore tooth. He'd gone back to look at her time and again, trying to figure out what had gone wrong.

At first he'd told himself that she'd been on the

periphery of one of his biggest kills and that was where the fascination lay, until he'd finally had the guts to recognise what he was feeling. Somehow, despite all the years of rigid discipline, in the moment when he'd first trained his binoculars on her face, he'd lost a part of himself and never wholly gotten it back. The fact that he'd felt anything at all had amazed and alarmed him; the habit of control had become so ingrained that he'd thought himself exempt from emotion. He'd tried to purge the feelings by having other women, but that hadn't worked.

He'd begun spending all his spare time watching her. For a while, given her youth and innocence, he'd even convinced himself he was guarding her. Another dry wisp of amusement curled his long, thin mouth. Guarding her. Oh, yeah, that was funny, he thought whimsically, when he was the guy straight out of her nightmares.

Now he was taking risks he wouldn't have believed himself capable of, exposing himself in ways he would never consider if he was on a professional assignment. But damned if he would just lie down and die quietly.

She didn't know he existed yet—much less *who* he was…although she had begun to feel his presence.

In the street, outside the cinema, three nights ago, she'd felt him watching her, had felt his intensity in the crosshairs settled on the creamy skin at the centre of her spine. He'd held the gun there, finger on the trigger...and it had been the closest he'd gotten to sex in a long time.

She was being watched. Roma stared at the building across from the hotel, a prickling tension crawling the length of her spine, for a moment oblivious to the wind whipping tendrils of hair across her cheek.

A lone gull wheeled above, its high, thin cry breaking the stasis. With a shake of her head, Roma forced her gaze from the impersonal smoked-glass frontage of the new hotel opposite, turned on her heel and walked back inside, wincing a little at her stiffness.

She probably *had* been watched...by any number of people—holiday-makers—simply occupying rooms. There was no need to get spooked about it.

She had to pull herself together. Her schedule for the next two days was hectic. Evan had organised a number of fund-raising events centred around the fashion world, designed to appeal to both the wealthy and the fashion conscious, and to attract maximum media attention. He'd gathered a number of celebrities, including well-known models and designers, and there had already been a storm of publicity. Tonight there was a reception, tomorrow a cocktail party. The week of activity would culminate in a fashion show and a ball, many of the events being held here at the hotel.

With any luck, she would be so busy she wouldn't have time to think, let alone feel.

Chapter 13

Ben escorted Roma to the reception, which was held at the hotel, using Charlie Speers as his backup.

He'd spent the day grimly going over the complications of forming a relationship with a woman he'd known for little more than a day, the sister of two of the best friends he'd ever had.

The whole exercise had been academic.

Something essential had shifted and settled inside him. His loss of control was an issue he still hadn't resolved, but the bottom line remained that he wanted Roma in his life, despite all the possible pitfalls. They would work out the details over time.

He'd gone through the motions of researching her past, read through some of the press releases surrounding the various crises the Lombard family had

weathered. Gradually he'd pieced together fragments
of information that confirmed what he already knew,
that Roma had lost more than a brother, she'd also
lost her career in child care and, to a large extent,
her freedom.

Even without the additional information, he'd already known what he had to do. He'd met Roma's
parents on a couple of occasions, and he liked and
respected them. He'd rung Roma's father and told
him what he intended. Guido Lombard hadn't been
impressed, but he'd been calmer than Ben had expected.

Once he'd hung up, he'd been impatient to get
Roma alone to consolidate his position, but achieving
that had proved to be impossible. The suite had been
overrun with people: Charlie, kicking his heels, hotel
security staff coming and going, delivering flowers
and invitations, diVaggio's people delivering clothes,
and Roma had actively avoided him, her gaze frosty.

He had hoped to get her alone tonight, but she'd
neatly evaded him. All evening he'd stayed close, his
frustration growing by degrees, but she'd kept moving, smiling, flirting, effortlessly charming. Women
liked her, the media loved her, and men dropped like
flies.

Her feminine understatement, that subtle air of
mystery, knocked them dead. He could see the moment it happened, the dazed expression followed by
a sharpening of male attention as they fell under her

spell. Then they checked him out…and took a step back.

Impatiently, he checked his watch and wondered how much longer they had to stay.

Roma accepted a glass of mineral water from a waiter, stiffening as McCabe's hand landed at her back, his thumb brushing the sensitive hollow of her spine just above the low-cut back of her dress. Casually, she moved away from him, turning so he couldn't pull the same trick again. If he tried, she would find a way to accidentally empty her glass of water where it was needed most.

McCabe was grimly handsome in a black dinner jacket that clung to his big shoulders, the crisp white shirt making his olive skin glow a dark, exotic gold. With his sleek, powerful build and the slash of the scar on his cheekbone, he looked like a panther walking among tabbies.

Despite his cool reserve, women flocked to McCabe, drawn by the palpable air of danger that hung about him, wanting to touch him, wanting to know who he was and how he'd gotten that sexy scar on his cheek. He'd stayed close all night, the perfect gentleman, the perfect attentive escort, opening doors for her, getting her food and drinks. The attention was disconcerting after he'd ignored her for the entire day. The last thing she wanted to be reminded of was the fact that last night she'd been happy for McCabe to touch her wherever he pleased.

One of Evan's tall celebrity models, who'd had a

little too much champagne, swayed up to McCabe and announced that she wanted to feel his muscles. McCabe eyed her with amusement, and when she pouted, he laughed, his teeth white against the stubbled darkness of his jaw.

Roma was transfixed by the byplay. She'd never seen McCabe laugh, and the abrupt change in his features was riveting. He looked relaxed, as lazily sensual as a big cat basking in the sun, and suddenly the lack of real intimacy between them struck her forcibly.

From the very first, apart from a blunt sexual appraisal, he'd shown little interest in her as a person. He'd been cool and gruff, extending her the barest courtesies. There had been no attempt to get to know her, no endearments or love words. He'd known she was a virgin and backed off initially, yet when they'd made love, the foreplay had been minimal, penetration quick and brutal. After that, he'd kept the formula simple; he had stayed on top of her all night.

She could remember his voice, a low soothing rumble, but she couldn't remember any actual words. Suddenly it was very important that she should have had those words, but the night had been hot and murky, and she'd drifted in and out of sleep, every memory blurred by the power and intensity and strangeness of making love for the first time.

If he'd shown the least bit of interest in her as a person when they'd woken, she would have been mindlessly happy, but he hadn't. He'd been aroused but matter-of-fact about having to postpone sex until he bought lubricant.

The model slid a finger along the lapel of McCabe's jacket, still pouting prettily. Roma's eyes narrowed on the gorgeous blonde and McCabe, and one word came to mind: rat.

She was confused, angry, miserable. Now she was jealous.

And she was in love with a rat.

She'd been denying it all day, sick to her stomach that after all these years she'd finally fallen in love, but with a man who had all the emotion of a chunk of granite and, when it came to sex, the practicality of a mechanic checking out a car engine.

She wondered if he'd bought lubricant today. She could almost wish he had; she knew just what she wanted to do with it, although McCabe might be a little surprised which orifice it ended up in.

Carefully, she set her drink down on a nearby table, made her excuses, then walked toward the ladies' room, keeping her gait steady. She had to get away, breathe air that didn't have McCabe in it, before she tossed her mineral water in his face.

That line from Shakespeare—"hell hath no fury like a woman scorned"—only began to describe how she felt.

Her jaw tightened. If her bodyguard had a hankering to check out any more car engines, he had plenty to choose from here. Hers had officially seized.

She waited for a few moments in the elegant anteroom, feeling suffocated by the heavily perfumed, overheated atmosphere. She left with a chattering group of ladies, then detached herself from them to walk briskly toward the large double doors of the ballroom, threading her way between groups of people and quickening her step as she went. Her dress was long and red, the skirt narrow, which made it hard to be inconspicuous, and she was wearing high heels, which impeded her progress, but she made it through the doors and out into the thickly carpeted foyer without attracting the attention of either McCabe or his sidekick, Charlie Speers.

She was almost at the elevator when something made her glance over her shoulder. McCabe was coming after her. Her stomach flipped in panic as she turned the final corner and grabbed a handful of skirt, hiking it up so she could walk faster. She reached the elevator, fumbled her key card out of her beaded purse, inserted it and stabbed in the code. The doors swished open just as McCabe called her name.

She stepped into the elevator and jabbed the button to close the doors, her heart thumping in her chest. McCabe's hand caught the doors just before they slid shut.

He stepped into the opening. "If you wanted to leave, you should have told me."

"The hotel's crawling with security. I didn't think there was much risk in going up to the suite. Besides, you were busy."

"I was with you."

"You're my bodyguard. You're paid to be with me."

"I changed the terms of the contract. I stopped being your bodyguard last night."

She eyed him coolly. "If you're no longer my bodyguard, then what are you doing here?"

"Protecting you, but I'm not doing it for money. I've put Alan and Charlie in place for backup."

There was a discreet cough behind them.

McCabe glanced over his shoulder. Charlie Speers and a member of the hotel security staff were standing just outside the elevator, looking vaguely embarrassed. McCabe acknowledged hotel security and dismissed Charlie for the night, then stepped into the elevator and hit the door control. Bare seconds later they stepped out of the lift, and he unlocked the door to the suite.

As soon as she got inside, Roma made a beeline for her room. She needed to think about McCabe's decision to withdraw from being paid to protect her. If that decision was motivated by a sense of pity or obligation, she would sooner call in a different firm to do the security.

She was just inside the door when McCabe spoke, halting her. "I rang your father today."

She turned slowly, hardly believing she'd heard right. "You did *what?*"

"I rang your father and told him we were involved."

For a moment, Roma wondered if there had been something alcoholic in the mineral water she'd been drinking. Or maybe it was McCabe who was drunk. "You told him we slept together?"

She adored her father, but he was definitely old-fashioned, old-school, and even less inclined for her to have anything to do with the male of the species than both her brothers put together.

"Not exactly."

She closed her eyes briefly. So, okay, the hit squad was on hold…for a few days at least. "*Why did you ring him*? What happened last night was between you and me, my family doesn't come into it."

"I rang him because your family trusted me to protect you, and I broke that trust." He shoved his hands into his pockets. "I'm sorry about today, but I had things to organise, things to think through."

Understanding dawned slowly. She'd thought he'd simply decided he'd made a mistake in getting involved with her, but it went deeper than that. "You had me checked out."

His gaze was cool, watchful. "I can't make a decision about any relationship without considering Bunny."

"Right. I'm a Lombard, and you've got a child to protect."

She saw the answer in his eyes and cut him off before he could speak. "Are you in love with me?"

He hesitated. "I want you in my life."

But he didn't want the trouble that went hand-in-hand with the Lombard family.

McCabe *did* want her, which was something. He wanted a relationship, which was more than she'd expected. But he wasn't anywhere near in love with her. Number one on his priority list was to protect his child. From her.

She knew it was an unfair assessment. That wasn't exactly what McCabe was doing, but it felt that way, and who could blame him? He had probably read about how she'd quit her job so she wouldn't put the children at risk. And no one who'd been involved in the hunt for Egan Harper, as he had been, could miss the fact that anyone hooking up with the Lombard family was fair game for terrorists. Jake's fiancée had died, and a few years later Gray's wife, Sam, had come close to being executed.

McCabe wanted her, but he wasn't anywhere near committed, and he wouldn't let her into his life—or anywhere near his daughter—until he was. That stung, despite the fact that she agreed with his need to protect Bunny. If she were in the same position, she would do exactly the same thing.

Her fingers clenched so tightly on her purse they began to ache, but she wasn't going to cry. She would be damned if she would cry.

She wanted it all and always had: marriage, babies, growing old together. For the first time in her life, she had glimpsed the possibility of that future for herself. She didn't know exactly what McCabe had glimpsed—wanting her in his life covered a lot of ground—but she did know one thing: *he* might be happy with half measures, but *she* never would be.

Her fingers found the edge of the door. ''Thanks for deciding you can be involved with me, but no thanks.''

The door snapped closed in Ben's face.

Ben turned the knob and met resistance. She'd locked him out.

His chest rose and fell. Slowly he released the knob and took a step back.

He'd made a mess of that.

Abruptly, he turned on his heel and strode out onto the terrace. The sea breeze cut through the heat of the night, sliding across his skin, sifting through his hair. He lifted his face to the wind and gripped the iron railing. It was late, but fading light still rimmed the horizon to the west, burnished copper slowly giving way to the glow of city lights. To the east, a huge yellow moon slid clear of the ocean to float, ponderous and belly-full, just above the smooth, flat surface of the water.

Turning, he leaned against the railing, arms folded across his chest as he stared broodingly into the lounge, and adjacent to that, his bedroom, with the big, empty king-size bed. The breeze drifted against his back, cooler now, so that the skin along his spine tightened.

He'd made mistake after mistake with Roma, although, looking back, he couldn't see how he could have reacted any differently. He'd had to be wary of getting involved with her—with any woman, for that matter. He had to consider his daughter's needs, and in this case, there were the added problems of the media attention and security risk associated with the Lombard family.

He would have to work damn hard to regain her trust, and he wasn't confident of the outcome. Something squeezed hard in his chest. For the first time in years, he felt completely at a loss with a woman. His first instinct was to batter down her door—and her defenses. But if he tried that angle, he would lose her for sure. He wasn't quite sure what he'd gotten in Roma—she was an odd, mystifying, fascinating personality—but he did understand that he was on the verge of losing something precious.

Abruptly, he turned, gripping the cold metal railing and drinking in the cool drift of air. The glitter of light off the hotel opposite captured his attention.

He frowned. The building gave him a cold itch up his spine. It was new, a smoked-glass monolith which had been constructed over the site of a set of older, much lower buildings, and it faced right into the Lombard suite. In security terms, it blew their protection out of the water. He would have a word with Gray about relocating the suite to the other side of the building or, better still, suggest he buy a secure house away from the hotel.

Chapter 14

For the next two days Roma was constantly escorted by McCabe. She became so used to his presence that she missed him when he wasn't near.

She knew what he was doing and could have protested, but the plain, miserable fact was that she wanted to be close to him. The only time they didn't spend together were the hours they slept, but even in sleep she was restlessly aware of him, waking often, and tossing and turning in the heat.

It was a seduction, and they both knew it. A cat-and-mouse game she was losing inch by inch as McCabe wore down her resistance.

The media loved it. Photographers and reporters hounded them, taking pictures, probing for information, wanting to know who the mystery man in her life was. It didn't take them long to find out that McCabe was a longtime friend of her brothers, and that he'd been a member of the Special Air Service team that had hunted down Egan Harper. The interest escalated, and all the old stories about the terrorist attacks were dug out and resurrected; speculation was rife.

Evan wasn't happy about the shift in publicity— he liked to be centre stage—but he was philosophical; the attention Roma and McCabe were getting would naturally spill over onto the charity functions.

Her father rang her on her mobile phone and threatened to come over early. Roma fended him off, reminding him that she was an adult. She was fine, and she was busy, and, in any case, the entire family would be there in two days' time for Evan's ball.

Her mother wasn't inclined to let it go when she came on the phone. Bridget Lombard was fiercely protective of all her children, and Roma knew she could sense that everything *wasn't* fine, but she let Roma have her way, promising to have a long talk with her when she got to the hotel.

Seconds after her mother had hung up, the phone rang again. This time it was Aunt Sophie. She didn't mince words.

"I hear you're sleeping with that big stud, Mc-Cabe."

Roma closed her eyes. Sophie was sixty-five going on thirty, a widow with no children. She'd had a very settled, staid marriage, but since her husband of over forty years had died, she'd been making up for lost time, determined to make the most of what she called her "twilight" years.

"Did you use protection?" Sophie demanded.

Roma rolled her eyes. "Yes."

"Good," she said with some satisfaction. "Then he hasn't got you pregnant yet." There was a pause, a fumbling sound, as if Sophie was checking to make sure no one was listening in. Her voice dropped to a husky whisper. "It was in the newspaper that you're shacked up with McCabe, but there's no sense in restricting yourself in this day and age. You want to give that nice blond boy a spin. What's his name? Charter. Play the field while you can, girl, before McCabe puts a ring on your finger."

There was a loud click, then silence. Sophie had hung up.

Roma slipped the phone back in her holdall and glanced around the room. The sun was shining, glinting prettily off the breakfast things on the dining table; a light breeze swirled through the potted shrubs and palms on the deck, filling the room with the rich scent of gardenias. McCabe and Alan were going over her itinerary, marking the route on a street map and discussing the locations, their voices a low rumble in the background. For a moment she was disoriented at the sheer normality of the scene, considering the conversations she'd just had.

Her parents knew she'd slept with McCabe, and now Sophie did, too, because she must have listened in. According to Sophie the newspapers were reporting that she was ''shacked up'' with McCabe.

In two days' time, when her entire family arrived to attend the ball, the odds were that every single member of her family would know she'd slept with McCabe.

She felt like crawling back into bed, pulling the covers over her head and telling everyone to go away and leave her alone.

She was twenty-four years old, and she'd been careful, even circumspect, with her relationships; then, the first time she slept with a man, the whole world found out.

McCabe's head lifted, as if he'd sensed her watching him. His gaze locked with hers.

Her stomach tightened on a jolt of pure feminine panic at the blunt male intent he made no effort to disguise. He was calmly, methodically, decimating her resistance, and she didn't know how much longer she could hold him off.

Several hours later McCabe escorted Roma from the studio of a television station, where she'd just finished taping an interview. Instead of walking toward the rental car they'd been using, he led her to his truck, which was parked beside the car.

Alan climbed out of the driver's seat, grinned good-naturedly at Roma and collected the keys for the rental.

McCabe opened the passenger door for her, but

when she tried to step in, her narrow skirt restricted her movement.

"Let me." McCabe's hands encircled her waist, the warmth of his fingers instantly penetrating the lightweight cream linen of her skirt and the much lighter silk of her blouse as he lifted her onto the passenger seat. He released her immediately and walked around to climb into the driver's seat.

Roma buckled herself in, still tingling from the pressure of his hands, and on edge as McCabe pulled out into traffic. She noticed he didn't seem to be heading back to the hotel. "Where are we going?"

"You're free for the afternoon, so I thought I'd take you to my gun club." He glanced at her. "If you don't want to do that, I'll take you back to the hotel."

"Why the gun club?"

He braked for a set of lights. "To show you how to shoot a gun."

For a moment she was so transfixed by what he'd said that she couldn't answer. "I know how to shoot a gun."

"Why doesn't that surprise me?"

Eventually McCabe pulled into what looked like a private country club. She looked around curiously as he pushed his door open and came around to help her down. This time she braced her hands on his shoulders. McCabe's eyes locked with hers as he lifted her from the seat. "Damn," he murmured as he set her down. "I'm getting tired of this."

He bent, and his mouth settled on hers, the kiss hot and hungry and slow.

A small, quivering moan of relief rose from deep in her belly as he gathered her close. He felt hot and hard against her, the scent of his body slightly sweaty and male in the afternoon humidity. He cupped her nape, massaging the sensitive skin while he tilted her head to deepen the kiss, groaning with satisfaction as she stretched out against him and wound her arms around his neck. When he finally released her, her legs felt like jelly and she had to clutch at his arms to get her balance.

"Maybe I should take you home right now," he said, shifting the hair from her shoulder and nuzzling her neck. "My place, where we can have some privacy, not that damn hotel."

She shivered as she felt the edge of his teeth on the curve of her neck and shoulder, the hot, wet stroke of his tongue. "You're taking a lot for granted, McCabe."

He lifted his head. "Maybe, but I haven't got time to do this any other way. Unless I can convince you otherwise, you're only here for a few days."

He bent, captured her mouth with his again, then released her and walked to the back of the truck to pull out a heavy nylon sports bag.

The shooting club was largely deserted, with just the odd enthusiast using the indoor facilities, which were split into booths with partitions, which had been designed to absorb sound.

McCabe placed the bag on a bench in the booth and shrugged out of his jacket. He extracted his handgun from the shoulder holster he was wearing over a white T-shirt and placed it in her hands.

"This is my weapon of choice, a Glock 19, semi-automatic. It's a nine millimetre, which means it packs plenty of stopping power. It takes a seventeen-shot magazine, and it'll kick back, but nothing you can't handle."

Roma examined the weapon. There was nothing flashy about the Glock; it was a plain matte-black and made almost entirely of composite material, with very little metal in its construction.

"I've used a nine millimetre before," she said, and then asked abruptly, "Why are you doing this?"

Years ago she'd had to pressure Blade to take her to his club and show her how to use a gun, and even though he'd eventually supplied her with a gun when she'd joined the club herself, neither of her brothers had wanted her to go near a weapon. They'd preferred that she knew nothing about weapons or combat, that she stayed at home and pretended no one was ever going to shoot at her or any member of her family.

McCabe handed her a pair of ear defenders. "A few nights ago you were in a combat situation. You have trouble sleeping…nightmares. I think you're suffering from something that's common to soldiers and cops—post-traumatic stress syndrome. It used to be called battle fatigue.''

He took a box of ammunition out of the bag and placed it on the bench. "I know how that feels. I've had my own nightmares to face. No one who has to deal with violence is immune from it.''

He shrugged out of the holster, then peeled his T-shirt off. There was a silvery puckered scar marring the bronzed flesh just above his hip. He turned and showed her two more on his back, then touched the scar on his cheek. "This one was the worst, because the knife that did this killed a friend and there wasn't a thing I could do to save him. Gray hauled my ass out of there before I got myself killed.''

"So this is therapy?''

He pulled his shirt back on. "Got any objections?''

For a moment she couldn't answer. McCabe was doing something nice for her—more, he was treating her as a person. If he had a male friend who suffered from the same problem, his solution would be the same. "No objections.'' She couldn't hide a smirk. "I just have to tell you that…I'm good.''

He went still. "How good?''

"So good you'll probably weep. Competition standard, although I don't compete.''

McCabe leaned against the wall, arms crossed as he studied her. "Now I *am* in love. Just how long have you been handling guns?''

"Since Jake died.''

"Figures. You didn't want to stay home, did you?"

She lifted the gun two-handed and sighted the target. The Glock was slightly lighter than the Sig. "I wanted to go out and shoot Harper."

"If it helps, I think you would have made a hell of a man."

"No kidding." Roma slid him a sideways look. "Are you laughing at me, McCabe?"

His mouth twitched. "Wouldn't dare."

"That's just as well, because it's a known fact that women don't need to be men. They're way too evolved."

"You won't get any argument from me."

"Good. Is it okay if I empty the clip?"

He placed his hand over his heart. "Baby, I thought you'd never ask."

She grinned and fitted the ear defenders, then checked out the target while McCabe settled his own ear defenders in place. The target was currently set for thirty feet, with an option to go to seventy-five. Thirty feet was a doddle; she'd been shooting one hundred and fifty since she was seventeen.

When the clip was empty, she ejected the magazine and began slotting in fresh shells.

McCabe reeled the target in. "You want thirty again?"

His voice was faint but audible. The ear defenders muffled sound; they didn't cut it out completely. "I'll go for the big time. Put it to seventy-five."

He grinned. "Oh, my beating heart. You can handle my weapon anytime."

"Cute, McCabe, very cute."

When she'd emptied the clip, he reeled the target in and gave a low whistle. "What do you normally shoot with."

"A Sig Sauer, P-226, with a laser sight."

"That's not a sporting weapon."

"No." She waited while he positioned another target. "It isn't."

Between shots, she rolled her shoulders, loosening the muscles. She wondered what McCabe really thought about her using a gun. He'd started out wanting to give her some therapy for Lewis's shooting and found out that she was more at home with a gun than any normal person would ever want to be. In a way, it defined her as a member of her family—and made her even less suitable girlfriend/wife/mother material.

Not for the first time, she wondered how much of her problem with even starting a relationship with a man was her own doing. It was easy to blame her family, and the security situation, for scaring men off, but she also had the attitude that if they ran that easily, she wasn't going to spend any time pining for them. She'd grown up with stresses and strains that weren't normal, and she found it difficult to relate to "normal" men. It was scary that the first time she'd ever been knocked off her feet by physical attraction would be with a man who was more at home with guns than she was, and had the bullet wounds to prove it.

McCabe stepped behind her. ''Sore here?''

His thumbs dug into the exact spot that ached between her shoulder blades. She almost moaned aloud at the release of tension. When he was finished, his arms came around her waist.

''Keep shooting.''

She sighted, squeezed off. The recoil nudged her back against his chest.

His arms tightened, steadying her; his breath stirred in her hair. ''I promised myself I wouldn't do this.''

He took off her ear defenders and tossed them onto the bench with his own. His arms tightened around her as he bent; his teeth fastened on her lobe. A hot shock wave of pleasure buckled her knees. McCabe caught her hard against him, a low growl of approval vibrating from deep in his throat. He nuzzled her neck. One big hand splayed over her belly, heavy and warm.

Roma fought the urge to turn in his arms and bury her mouth against his. Her heart was slamming in her chest; she was hot and trembling, her hands shaking. ''I'm not going to hit anything at this rate.''

''Just shoot, baby.''

This time she leaned into McCabe while she squeezed off, letting him absorb the recoil. The solid jut of his arousal rubbed against the cleft of her bottom, making her even hotter than she already was. "I thought you were supposed to be rubbing my back?"

She could almost feel his grin.

"I had a better idea."

His hands slid up over her rib cage, cupped her breasts, the heat of his palms burning through the silk and the lacy bra beneath. Her hands jerked; the next shot went wild.

She bit into her bottom lip, aiming for dead centre. His thumbs rubbed over her nipples. The gun jerked again, but she waited it out. He nuzzled the sensitive hollow beneath her ear, the hot stroke of his tongue made her shiver. This time she hit the neighbouring target.

He lifted his head. "Having trouble?"

"I was in the ball park."

"On the wrong target."

"I didn't think you were watching."

"With you, I'm always watching." He undid a button of her blouse and slipped his hand inside.

Her breath came on a rasp. "If I can't hit anything, it's because my instruction's suspect."

He took the gun from her. "Your instruction was lousy."

Methodically, he filled the clip, snapped it into place, then took up his stance, all his actions performed with a slick economy of movement. He could probably have done it blindfolded, and taking into account his years in the SAS, he had most likely trained to operate in pitch-blackness.

The stench of cordite filled the air. When he was finished, he put the gun down. "Now you do it. This time I promise I'll behave."

Roma picked up the gun, released the magazine and began slotting shells.

His arms came around her again when she began firing. "McCabe, you're a bare-faced liar."

"I said I'd behave," he murmured. "I didn't say how. And considering what I'm about to do to you, you should start calling me Ben."

She closed her eyes, took a deep breath. "And just what is it that *you think* you're going to do to me?"

He told her in blunt terms exactly what he had in mind. Roma swallowed, placed the gun carefully on the bench and turned in his arms. A girl could only stand so much.

"But I'll do whatever you want," he said quietly. "Just tell me."

She had the sudden urge to reach up and cup his face, rub her hands over the stubble that darkened his jaw, then rise up on her toes and press her mouth against his. Just the thought of reaching for him sent a sharp ripple of awareness through her. He'd made no bones about the fact that he wanted her. It wasn't enough, but she was beginning to despair of ever having what she wanted. It had to be better than the relationship desert she'd lived in for years. The trick was to try not to have expectations.

With a sigh, she rose up. She wound her arms around his neck and kissed him. It was surrender and she knew it, had known it when she kissed him out by the truck, but she didn't care. "I give up. I surrender. You win."

She felt his hands in her hair, cupping her head. He eyed her warily. "And what does that mean, exactly?"

"It means, okay, we'll try it your way. For a while."

"Does that mean you'll stay with me?"

"Are you asking?"

"Yeah, I'm asking."

A muscle throbbed along his jaw; abruptly his mouth fastened on hers. He crowded her back against the wall and she hummed with pleasure, stretching and rubbing herself against him as the long, drugging kiss continued. She felt a tug on her blouse, then a button went flying. Her bra loosened, and she shuddered as he took her breast into his mouth, aching heat bursting through her as his tongue worked the nipple, drawing strongly so that she climaxed and sagged, dazed, in his hands.

He said something low and rough beneath his breath. She felt his hands working her skirt up until it was bunched around her waist, the tug as he pulled her panties down her legs. The rush of air circulating around her bare bottom was vaguely shocking as she leaned limply against the partition and watched as he took a foil packet from his pocket, shoved his jeans down far enough to free his arousal, then calmly sheathed himself.

Tension settled in the pit of her stomach. She knew condoms were practical, safe, and anyone with any brains should use them, but somehow the mechanics of putting the condom on put their lovemaking in context. Despite her surrender, McCabe wasn't lost on a tide of passion, and he wasn't going to make the mistake of making love to her without protection.

She wound her arms tightly around his neck as he lifted her so that her feet were dangling inches from the floor and pinned her back against the wall. "Wrap your legs around my waist and hold on."

Awkwardly, she closed her legs around his waist and slung one arm around his neck while she dragged up his T-shirt. The white interlock was half way up his belly when he began penetrating her.

The drag of latex against her delicate inner flesh registered. Her fingers dug into his shoulders as he thrust short and sharp, working himself inside her in steady increments.

She didn't like the condom.

The layer of latex was thin, but somehow dehumanising, rasping her nerve endings so that she quivered with each thrust, growing more and more unhappy.

Despite that, her body responded helplessly, the hot tingling excitement taking her over so that she clung to McCabe, heart pounding, breasts tight and throbbing where they pressed against the muscular wall of his chest.

Sultry heat seemed to explode in the room, so that it was hard to breathe, and her clothes, twisted and uncomfortable, clung damply to her skin where they touched. Her breasts exposed where her blouse swung open, the rough texture of the wall scraped against her bare bottom, and one of her shoes dangled from her toe, then dropped with a little thud to the floor. The other shoe was still firmly on. Somehow that detail was distressing.

The percussion of shots echoed, startling her. That meant that somebody else had entered the range and was using a booth. Someone strolled by, the top of a dark head visible over the stall door. If the person had been taller, he would have seen in.

Misery and pleasure combined, twisted through her. If McCabe was lost to passion, maybe the unsettling feeling of exposure wouldn't matter so much, but his expression was closed.

He was expert at making love, an expert at making her *feel.*

Already he knew her body intimately, knew exactly how to touch her so that she was helpless in his grasp. She felt him glide deep. The sensation shoved her over the edge and she began to climax

again, tears seeping from beneath her lids as she
clenched her jaw to keep from making any sound.
McCabe watched her from between lowered lids,
prolonging her climax until she sagged against his
chest. He continued to move inside her, more easily
now because she'd climaxed twice, until finally she
felt him pulsing deep inside her, and yet that, too,
seemed cold and controlled because he wasn't truly
touching her.

She wanted him to touch her.

She didn't want him to wear a condom, and she
didn't want that cold control.

And the thought of making love without a condom
and risking pregnancy didn't scare her the way it
should.

Stricken, she examined her feelings. They were
deep and painful, and they weren't going away, no
matter how much she tried to fight them. When he'd
touched her, pushed her up against the wall, she'd
shivered with relief because she'd wanted him so.
She hadn't been capable of refusing him, and she
hadn't cared where they were, let alone that anyone
might walk in and find them.

She had wanted him to touch her, hold her, make
love to her. Instead, they'd had sex against a wall.

Seconds later McCabe withdrew and set her down
on her feet. She stumbled slightly, because her legs
were so wobbly, and she had one shoe on and one
off. He steadied her as she fumbled her skirt down

over her hips and righted her clothes. She searched, without success for the button off her blouse. Mc-Cabe found the button, then bent and fitted the dropped shoe to her foot.

He retrieved her panties, and she slipped them on, but the feeling of dampness was uncomfortable. She needed a shower and a change of clothes, a chance to get her composure back.

A short time later he escorted her from the gun club and out into the car park, his hand firm on the small of her back. Although escorted was the wrong word. It felt more like being herded by a hungry stallion. She felt dazed, light-headed, dazzled by the blazing sunlight as she kept pace with him, clutching the gaping lapels of her blouse together where the button was missing.

It must have rained earlier, because everywhere was wet, and steam lifted from the dark asphalt, wrapping her in moist heat so that she was instantly dewed with perspiration.

She was throbbing and tingling inside, her legs still unsteady. The wind swirled, hot and steamy, flipping at her skirt and blowing up between her legs, making her acutely aware of the dampness between her thighs.

McCabe lifted a hand, and she saw with mortification that Alan was leaning against his car, dark glasses shading his eyes as he tracked their progress.

Even though she was fully dressed, she felt as vulnerable as if she were naked, as if what they'd just done was imprinted all over her, from her tangled hair to the missing button of her blouse and her crumpled linen skirt.

Logically, her mussed hair and clothing didn't matter on the scale of things, but her dishevelment somehow underlined her utter lack of control in this relationship.

What truly mattered was that McCabe hadn't said he loved her.

Chapter 15

Later on that evening, Ben picked up a call while Roma showered and dressed. Reception had a delivery for Miss Lombard.

Minutes later, one of the hotel security staff delivered a heavy envelope with Roma's name written on it in pen.

Ben turned the big envelope over in his hands. There was nothing to indicate who had sent it. He slit the brown manila and saw what he expected, a thick wad of photos—probably from diVaggio.

With a grunt, he tossed it down on the coffee table and went to get his own shower; they were already running late.

* * *

Roma perched on the couch and reached for the envelope, emptying the contents onto the smooth surface of the coffee table.

Leaning forward, she began to flip through the stack of black-and-whites. She frowned. She'd assumed Evan had sent her some prints of his designs, or the fashion shoot she'd done the day before, but these obviously hadn't come from him. There had been photographers at all of the fund-raising venues, but whoever had taken these shots hadn't been interested in the new cancer ward. All the photos were of her and McCabe just strolling around.

She began to recognise all the places they'd been in the past couple of days, the different places they'd parked, the café where they'd grabbed a sandwich. The gun club earlier that afternoon.

Her stomach tightened with unease as she looked at photo after photo of McCabe with his hand on the small of her back. McCabe lifting her into the truck. McCabe kissing her.

Someone was watching them, shadowing their every move. Something about the photos made her frown, but she couldn't quite put her finger on what was wrong.

"What is it?"

Roma glanced up, and her heart did an automatic flip-flop in her chest. McCabe was dressed all in black, the clothes stark, expensive, the jacket cut to hide the bulge of a shoulder holster. With the cool blue glitter of his eyes and the lash of the scar on his cheekbone, he looked big and dangerous and sexy.

"Someone's been taking photos."

Ben sat beside her on the couch, took a pen out of his pocket and used it to spread the photographs out along the surface of the table, examining each one in turn. His mood turned grim.

None of the photos in themselves were overtly threatening, but their mere existence was ominous. The person who'd sent the photos had wanted to make a bold statement. He was flaunting his knowledge, his power. He'd been following Roma. And now he was cocky enough to tell them about it. "Have you got any idea who might have sent these?"

"No."

Ben hadn't expected Roma to say anything else. Whoever had taken the photos had a serious problem in the head department. If it was the same guy who'd shot at her friend in Sydney, then they had big-time trouble, although there was nothing to link these photos with the shooting.

The photographs themselves were good, professional, which didn't mean a great deal in itself; there were plenty of camera buffs around. But all the same, he would get the police to run a check on all the photographers who'd been covering the fund-raising events. He would use his own people to find out where the photos had been processed; there weren't that many places in town that specialised in developing prints of this size and quality, and in this much of a hurry.

He looked at the series taken at the gun club car park, and cold resolve settled in his gut. Whoever had taken these photos had gotten close. *Too* close. If he came that close again, they would nail him.

First he would brief Gray; then he would start calling in some favours of his own.

Ben picked up his cell phone and stabbed in a short code. When the receiver was finally lifted, the voice that answered was thick with sleep and little more than a grunt.

"Rawlings."

"What took you so long?"

Carter groaned. "I love you, too, sweetheart. What's the time?" He bit out a rusty string of curses when he found out just what time it was. "I'm on leave," he said in a quietly outraged voice. "I've just spent three months crawling through wet, snake-infested jungle, and you—"

"I'm doing protection for Roma Lombard," Ben cut in. "I need you for some offensive surveillance."

There was a moment of silence, then a gravelled curse.

Ben briefly outlined the situation. "I need West, too, if I can get him. Do you know where he is?"

Carter grunted. "I'll get West. We were on the same rotation and got airlifted back together. After three months in that hell-hole, we were due some R and R.''

''This won't be a picnic, Carter.''

''I know, I know,'' Carter mumbled, his voice distracted, as if he was searching for clothes. ''It'll probably be boring, hiding behind potted plants and playing with microphones, but what the heck, it's what I do. Besides, I really want to meet the guy who thinks he can hassle Roma Lombard while he still has a face.''

Carter jockeyed his four-wheel drive beneath the covered entrance of the Lombard Hotel.

West surveyed the gleaming sports cars and limousine ahead of them, the bustle of uniformed porters and valets double-timing it at the impressive entrance. ''Maybe you should have considered washing your heap before bringing it here?''

Carter eyed West tolerantly. West was a city boy, so he forgave him for calling his truck a heap. Besides, West had his own weaknesses. In his spare time he obsessed over Norton bikes and clapped-out Jags. Any time Carter wanted revenge, all he had to do was lift the garage door on West's equally clapped-out Victorian doer-upper. ''If I wash this baby, I'll have to realise it's got a serious rust problem, and when I realise that, I'll have to do something about it.''

''Yeah, it's called buying a vehicle that does what it's supposed to do without argument and is environmentally friendly into the bargain. Look how much smoke's billowing out of the exhaust. We can hardly see that old guy now.''

Carter looked in the direction West indicated. ''We can't see him because it's dark.''

West shook his head. ''He's started coughing.''

Carter killed the engine. It died with a spluttering groan that made him feel like patting the dash.

The porter was wheezing asthmatically and blowing his nose as they strode up the steps. ''That's a bad cough you got there,'' Carter said, smiling and handing over the keys so the guy could park the truck. ''You should think about seeing a doctor.''

The receptionist glanced up as two men approached her desk. The blond guy easily topped six feet, and was wearing jeans and a T-shirt that didn't do much to hide any of the hard-packed muscle beneath. He was deeply tanned, his Viking-blond mane streaked a startling silver by the sun, light blue eyes glittering in a face that was tough and leanly handsome. The dark guy wasn't as tall, but of the two, he looked the more dangerous. He had big shoulders and whipcord-lean hips, and walked with a sinuous, catlike grace. He was dressed casually in black jeans and a black V-neck T-shirt made of some gauzy material, his sleek shoulders gloved by a loose jacket that had probably cost six months of her salary. A dark fall of silky hair framed a face that was both dangerous and beautiful, the hard, square jaw softened by a mouth that was full and frankly sensual, his eyes arresting slits of amber.

She wondered dreamily if she was hallucinating, or maybe she'd somehow got caught in the middle of one of those underwear ads. If she was dreaming, she didn't want to wake up anytime soon. The blond guy was mouth-wateringly gorgeous, the dark guy lean and dangerous and panther-sleek. She didn't know who to lust over the most.

The blond guy leaned on the desk and smiled, white teeth flashing against his dark jaw. "We're looking for Roma Lombard's suite."

Roma Lombard. Understanding filtered slowly into her oxygen-impaired mind. She remembered the instruction that had been phoned down by that other brooding stud Ms. Lombard had up there.

Both of the men flashed IDs. Absently she noted the details, matched faces, operating purely on instinct. She explained that security would have to escort them to the suite, then watched as two tight, world-class butts sauntered away from her, only remembering to alert security as they disappeared from sight.

When she'd terminated the call, she sighed, leaned on the desk and dropped her chin into one hand. She'd never wanted to be rich before and had always felt a little sorry for the troubles the Lombard family had had to face because of their wealth, but she could see where money would have its uses.

As soon as she got off work, she was going to buy

a lottery ticket. If she won, she knew exactly what she would buy first.

Ben opened the door and let Carter and West in.

"Where's Roma?" Carter demanded immediately.

Roma rose from the couch, grinning. "Carter?"

Ben's jaw tightened as Carter strode over and pulled Roma into his arms. "If you're finished with the touching reunion, let's get down to business."

Carter's head came up, his stare cool and measuring. Ben ignored West's thoughtful expression.

With slow, careful movements, Carter set Roma away from him and backed off a step.

Roma glanced at Ben. "What's the matter?"

"It's all right," Carter said soothingly. "I just didn't realise."

"Realise what?"

"That I was stepping on someone's toes."

Ben felt some of the tension inside him ease. Carter had backed off. Maybe he was just being friendly with Roma; with Carter it was hard to tell what was really going on beneath the surface, but playing or serious, the man was pure hell on women, and Ben didn't share. Now West and Carter both knew to keep their hands off.

West bent and gave Roma a brotherly peck on the cheek, slid a glance at Ben, lifted a brow, then strolled over to the couch. Ben felt his frustration mount. He knew that Carter and West had spent time with the Lombard family, and both were obviously at ease with Roma. He had to wonder just how many more men he was going to have to warn off.

West began perusing the photographs on the coffee table as they all sat down. "The resolution's good," he said slowly. "He's using different lenses to get different effects—he likes the equipment. He's cool, methodical, a regular camera buff." He examined the photos taken in the car park outside the gun club and frowned. "He got in close here. That's not consistent with the other shots."

"Tell me about it. Our man suddenly turned into a risk taker." Ben pulled the envelope with the details of the Sydney shooting from beneath the spread-out photos. "There's another problem." He handed the envelope to Carter. "I don't know if this is related. I hope not, but we have to consider it."

Carter pulled the report from the envelope and quickly scanned the first page. His blue gaze turned cold. He glanced at Roma. "Someone tried to shoot you?"

"Someone shot into a crowd," she amended. "I wasn't the one who got hurt."

Carter passed the report to West.

West flipped through the sheets, paused on the last page, then began looking at the black-and-whites. "He used a sniper rifle."

Roma eyed him coolly. "That doesn't mean he's a sniper."

West placed the report on the coffee table. "If someone was shooting at me with ammunition of a calibre that was consistent with a sniper rifle, I'd assume he was a sniper. Better that than to underestimate the shooter and wind up dead.''

Carter picked up one of the photos that had arrived that afternoon. ''Even without the shooting, these photos are threat enough and, happening so close to the shooting, there is the possibility that they're linked. I wouldn't take the chance that they're not. Have you brought the police in yet?''

Ben leaned forward in his chair. That was the value of Carter and West. They were coming into this cold, with no preconceptions. ''The police are investigating, but they don't have a lot to go on. And whether there's an overt threat or not is immaterial. It's Roma's safety that counts.''

Roma looked up from the photos she'd been perusing. ''What if it isn't *my* safety that's at stake?'' she said quietly. ''I'm not the one who's at the centre of most of the shots.''

West studied the photos she'd pointed out, stroking his chin. ''She's right.'' He glanced at Ben. ''You're the subject.''

Ben frowned. ''That doesn't make sense.''

''It does if the Sydney shooting is linked,'' Carter said slowly. ''Roma wasn't hurt, it was the guy with her who collected the bullet. In the photos, you're the guy with Roma. If the two incidents *are* linked, there's your motivation.''

''It's still damned nebulous.''

Carter shrugged. ''Maybe, but don't forget, we're

dealing with the Lombard family here. This isn't the first time someone has tried to mess them around.'' He smiled faintly in Roma's direction.

Roma caught Ben's gaze. ''Maybe those photos are linked with the shooting and maybe they're not, but why take chances?''

West relaxed back into the soft hide couch. ''I agree with Roma. Why take chances? Carter's right. She wasn't the one who got shot in Sydney. It was the boyfriend.''

Ben met West's gaze for a long moment. He wasn't comfortable with what they were saying, but he had a lot of respect for West's judgement. His insight was sharp, his instincts spooky. ''So, what do you suggest?''

''What's the itinerary?''

Ben briefly outlined the schedule for the next two days.

''Cancellation,'' West murmured. ''Or else get yourself some body armour.''

''In thirty degrees? I'll die of heat stroke.''

Carter sprawled back in his chair and stretched out his legs. ''But you'll die a hero. Think of the head-lines.''

''Believe me, I am,'' Ben muttered as he uncoiled himself from the couch. He strolled to the fridge and extracted a six pack of beer. ''Any more bright ideas?''

West twisted the lid off his bottle. ''Yeah. If you need a Lombard for the fund-raiser, how about substituting Blade? He's pretty enough, and you'd need a silver bullet to kill him.''

Ben grinned. ''A substitute's not a bad idea, but I don't see him in one of diVaggio's dresses. He doesn't shave his legs.''

Carter snickered, and Roma rolled her eyes. ''A substitute's out of the question. And apart from the publicity angle, Evan's designed a whole range of clothing specifically for me. Maybe you haven't noticed, but I'm not that tall. If I cancel, he won't be able to get another model on short notice.''

A phone buzzed. Ben and West both reached inside their jackets.

''It's mine.'' Roma pulled her cell phone from her evening bag and got to her feet. ''It's Evan,'' she said as she strolled toward her room. ''Probably wondering why we're not at the dinner.''

Ben eyed the sleek, slim phone in West's hand. ''That's new.''

West tossed the phone to Ben. ''I designed it, along with a couple other devices. Telephone company's after me now.''

''That means you're either dead or rich.''

West smiled lazily. ''I didn't choose death.''

Carter put his empty beer bottle on the table. ''Sold his soul to the devil instead, signed on the dotted line and took a chunk of shares. Now he's in deep with Gray and Blade.''

Ben tossed the phone back to West.

West caught it and slipped it into the inside pocket of his jacket. ''I went into partnership with Gray and

Blade," he said in answer to Ben's raised brows. "Designing communication equipment and special forces weaponry." He picked up his beer. "Now the Libyans are after me."

"Speaking of partnerships," Carter murmured, eyeing Ben, "what's going on with you and Roma?"

"We're in a relationship."

West looked at Ben, arrested. If anyone was relationship-shy, it was Ben. His ex-wife, Nicola, was a beautiful woman, but she'd burned him all the way through. She'd liked the uniform and the mystique of the SAS, but whenever Ben was away, and that was a lot, she hadn't stayed at home, either. When she'd left Ben high and dry with his baby daughter, she'd already been pregnant with some other guy's child. "I can't blame you," he said slowly. "She's gorgeous, but…" He shook his head. "*Roma Lombard.* You're buying into a complicated load of trouble."

"It's trouble," Ben agreed. "But there's nothing complicated about it."

"Yeah," Carter chipped in. "Those big brothers of hers pretty much simplify the equation. Gray plus Blade equals maiming. If you're lucky, death. Either one of them could kill you in his sleep. Then there are all those millions of dollars."

"I'm not interested in her money."

"Mate, whether you want the money or not is academic. It's there."

Ben broke out another beer for Carter. "I didn't plan to get involved."

"Who does?" West said laconically.

The odd note in West's voice caught Ben's attention. "You still married, West?"

"Last time I heard." He paused. "Tyler got her doctorate last year."

"Have you seen her lately?"

"Not lately." He lifted his beer, trailed one long finger down the moisture condensed on the bottle. "I went to her graduation."

Carter sat bolt upright on the couch. "You did *what?*"

"She didn't see me."

"Then why in hell did you go?"

West shrugged. "I was in town."

Carter frowned. "Don't do it again," he said quietly. "Next time you get the urge, ring me. I'll save you from yourself."

A rare smile slid across West's mouth. "What if I don't want to be saved?"

Carter picked up his beer. "Too bad, I'll damn well save your useless hide anyway."

Ben glanced toward Roma's room. He could just catch the faint murmur of her voice. She was still tied up with diVaggio, which didn't surprise him. The man loved to talk. He reached for his beer, listening to the desultory wrangling between Carter and West. Despite years of friendship, Ben still didn't know that much about West, past or present. He was the proverbial dark horse—a strange mixture of wild risk and icy control. His quiet manner, the lazy, indolent way he moved, were deceptive. When a situation turned fluid, there was no one better to have at your back, but outside of the military, West was an enigma, his private life utterly private. From all accounts, he lived like a monk. If he'd had a girl-friend since leaving his wife, Ben hadn't heard about it.

Carter yawned and set down his empty bottle. "So what event's happening tomorrow?"

"A fashion show. You equipped for it?"

"I'm equipped—unless you need a rocket launcher. That might take a coupla days."

"I'm not talking weaponry."

A gleam of amusement entered West's eyes. "The idea is that you have to blend in."

Carter looked quietly appalled. "Oh, jeez." He levelled a stare at West. He'd never seen any man with more clothes than West, and that included Blade, who was a walking clothes-horse. He had to own something Carter could fit into.

West held up his hands in justifiable self-defence. "Uh-uh, forget it. I've seen what you do to clothes. Besides, you're too big. You'd wreck my jackets."

Ben decided to put Carter out of his misery. "I've got a jacket you can borrow."

Carter stared gloomily at his empty bottle. "Just as long as I don't have to carry one of those male handbags."

"Cheer up," Ben murmured. "If you get to carry a handbag, you can always put your gun in it."

Chapter 16

From his vantage point backstage, Ben eyed the sea of people crushed into the auditorium, his unease mounting. The crowd was swollen by media people and television crews; there were cords running all over the place, and one of the aisles was mostly blocked with people in wheelchairs. Because of the heat, all the doors were open, further compromising the security, and people were clustered around them, enjoying the faint breeze.

He rolled his shoulders, trying to ease the tension in his spine and dissipate some of the heat that prickled his skin. The body armour was lighter and less bulky than the older type, which had ceramic inserts, but the extra layer was still killing him. He was tempted to take it off, not totally convinced that he was a target, but Roma had been fiercely insistent that he wear it. And if that was what it took to make her happy and to lessen some of the tension those photos had caused, then he would damn well wear it.

He spoke into his lip microphone, checking in with his people. Carter and West were each running a group, monitoring areas they'd identified earlier on as prime spots for anyone to set up a shot. The rationale behind offensive surveillance was to not wait for an attacker to come in close but to actively search for anyone who looked suspicious, then move in and check them out. So far they'd managed to tick off a significant proportion of the audience, but then, they weren't here for the sake of popularity.

DiVaggio wasn't happy, but he'd calmed down when Ben had given him his choice: he accepted the security, or Ben removed Roma from the show.

The police had searched everyone carrying a camera, but other than that, their presence was low-key. This was, after all, a charity event attended by the well-heeled and the well-known, hardly a venue for a riot.

Ben turned his attention backstage, automatically running his gaze loosely over the seething mass of models dressing and undressing, the make-up people, and hairdressers and sundry other hangers-on, using his peripheral vision to pick out anything that didn't fit. It all fit, he decided grimly: utter chaos.

A model swayed in off the catwalk to the strains

of classical music, and another strolled on, but Ben scarcely noticed as the makeshift curtain behind him, which he'd rigged up so that Roma could have some privacy changing, was twitched aside and she moved past him to wait her turn, face pale as she met his gaze, her expression calm, almost blank.

She hadn't said anything, but he knew what it was costing her to walk out in front of that sea of people every time. She'd been shaken by those damn photos.

Earlier that day Ben had tracked down the firm that had done the processing, but he'd come up with close to nothing. The transaction had been carried out by an intermediary, a teenage kid they hadn't been able to trace. Payment had been made in cash. That information had sent a chill down Ben's spine. Another layer, another mystery. Their photographer might be a risk taker, but he wasn't sloppy with details.

He watched as Roma walked out onto the catwalk. He had to restrain himself from grabbing her and carrying her away, and the hell with diVaggio. If she'd shown any signs of panic, he wouldn't have hesitated.

For the first time Ben paid attention to what she was wearing...or wasn't wearing. The dress consisted of pieces of metallic fabric strung together with tiny chains. If there was a major design factor in the dress, it was fresh air. His jaw clamped. Next time he got diVaggio alone, he was going to wrap his hands around his throat and squeeze.

The whole room went quiet when Roma was on the catwalk. She was muscled and sleek, with the tensile elegance of a cat. It didn't matter what she was wearing; the clothes were simply props. She had charisma, star quality, call it what you will. There were more physically impressive women there, but none of them created the jaw-dropping hush that she did.

A man surged to his feet directly in front of Roma, a camera in his hands. Ben saw Roma freeze a split second before West was on the man, felt his own raw flare of panic.

"Son of a bitch," he ground out from between clenched teeth. That was it; as far as Roma was concerned, the fashion show was over. DiVaggio could weep and plead, but he'd be damned if Roma was walking out there again.

Static hissed in his ear as West checked in. The photographer had already been searched once; now he was suing.

"Tell him to get in line," Ben muttered as Roma walked past and was immediately engulfed by diVaggio and a crowd of dressers.

"Get her out of here," West said flatly.

Ben went still. "What's wrong?"

"A feeling."

Ben swore coldly, fluently, ignoring the amused stare of an almost-naked model. If West had a "feeling," you could bet the farm on it.

He shouldered past a gaggle of hairdressers and

make-up professionals, racks of gowns, more models. Roma was at the centre of the chaos, being helped into a white gown with a full skirt. Ben felt as though he'd just been kicked in the chest; she was wearing a wedding dress. "I need to talk to you."

"I'm about to take a walk down the aisle."

Roma held still while her hair was twisted up into a knot and pinned. Inside, she was still shaking from the moment when the photographer had jumped to his feet. For a split second she hadn't seen a camera in his hands, she'd seen a gun. She'd frozen, but not with fear; fury had flashed through her. Then West had flowed into the picture and grabbed the camera, and she'd forced herself to move. She must have gone through all the required motions, but she had no actual memory of doing so. When she'd walked backstage and seen Ben standing coolly watching her, his expression rock-steady and controlled, she'd calmed down. Despite the threat that hung over them, she'd never felt physically safer than when she was with Ben.

"Let someone else do it," he said bluntly. "I want you out of here."

DiVaggio eyed Ben coolly. "No one else can wear the wedding dress."

Roma met Ben's gaze. She knew what was going through his mind. He thought she was scared. "I'm okay," she said calmly. "And this is the last dress." She wasn't going to let fear or threats stop her from doing what she wanted ever again. The need for security would always be there, but she wasn't going to let it put a stranglehold on her life.

Someone pinned a drift of some gauzy fabric in her hair, anchoring it with a wreath of white rosebuds and dark green leaves. A matching bouquet was thrust into her hands. A tall, blond male model dressed in a morning suit appeared, ready to act as escort. The first strains of the wedding march played.

McCabe moved in, blocking the model. His hand settled at her back, the heat from his palm burned through the white silk as he urged her forward. "The hell with this," he said curtly. "If you're going out there, I'm escorting you."

She dug in her heels, refusing to move. "No."

One of the make-up girls looked Ben up and down and grinned appreciatively. In a fitting black T-shirt, black pants and black body armour, his gun holstered at his thigh, McCabe looked as if he'd just walked out of a war zone. "The crowd'll love it. Everyone knows he's not a model."

Evan eyed McCabe icily. "What are you trying to do, McCabe, ruin my show?"

Ben's expression was cold enough that Evan backed up a step. "My priority is Roma. If I'd had my way, she wouldn't be here at all."

The breath hissed from between Evan's teeth. With an impatient gesture, he leaned forward and pulled the veil down over her face. "Go!"

Roma resisted, glaring into Ben's face "I don't want you walking out there with me."

"And I don't want you walking out there at all. It's your call. Are we doing this, or do we leave?"

Her jaw squared. "We're doing it, but if anything happens to you, McCabe, *I'm* going to kill you."

She caught the edge of his grin as he propelled her forward. "As long as it's in bed."

"It won't be if you hustle me down the catwalk like you're taking me into custody. You have to hold my arm…like this."

"Anyone ever tell you you're bossy?"

When they strolled onto the catwalk, the crowd went wild, the applause rising in a wave.

"They know you're my bodyguard."

"That's not what the newspapers are saying," he muttered, restlessly scanning the crowd as they approached the end of the catwalk. "How quickly can we get this done and get out of here?"

Roma saw West glide to the end of the catwalk at floor level, his back to them as he stood motionless, oblivious to the displeasure of the audience, head up as he stared across the sea of faces. "Hold my hand here. I have to turn around, then you lift my veil. You haven't got the ring, so you'll just have to pretend to slip it on my finger."

After she'd turned, careful of the full skirt, Roma came back to stand directly in front of McCabe, as if they were exchanging vows. Obediently he picked up her left hand and slid the imaginary ring onto her finger with about the same amount of ceremony he used when he slotted the clip into his gun.

"Now you have to kiss me," she prompted.

His gaze flicked past hers and out over the audience. "Were you going to kiss that male model?"

"Just put your lips on mine, McCabe, and hurry up."

"You were," he muttered. "Damn, I'm gonna kill diVaggio." He lifted the veil, framed her face with his hands and laid his mouth on hers.

Despite her tension, pleasure shivered through her at the brief caress.

Abruptly, Ben broke the kiss. "Okay, let's scoot."

The applause rolled and built, breaking over them in a heavy cascade of sound. Cameras flashed, half blinding her. Ben swore as the crowd came to its feet, his hand locked around her wrist.

A shot snapped through the thunderous applause. Roma was jerked backward, her gown wrapping around her legs, veil tumbling over her face as she half twisted, hands flung out to break the fall. Time seemed to slow, stop, as she lay sprawled on her side, tangled in folds of white silk, the smothering length of gauze shrouding her vision; then normal time snapped back in. Ben had been shot.

Her heart slammed into overdrive. Roma knew he had body armour on, but the knowledge was academic. He had been *shot*.

She dragged the veil from her face, tossed it aside and yanked at the dress until she could crawl to where McCabe was lying on his back, his eyes closed.

Fear made her clumsy as she crouched over him, shielding him while she searched for a wound. He was breathing, his mouth slightly parted, his chest rising and falling.

She tore at the tabs of the body armour, fingers fumbling as the Velcro snagged, and shoved it enough aside that she could slide her hand beneath the layers of Kevlar. His T-shirt was damp and clung to his skin. Feverishly, she jerked the T-shirt loose from his pants and shoved her hand beneath, needing the direct contact. Heat blasted from his skin, and his belly twitched as she pushed higher over his rib cage, to the centre of his chest. His heart thudded against her palm, strong and steady. The relief barely registered as she slid her hand over the broad width of his chest, expecting at any moment to feel the wet seep of blood, the raw opening of a wound.

Her gaze caught on a perforation in the dull, black Kevlar sheathing his chest, and she went still.

McCabe *had* been shot in the chest. The body armour had stopped the bullet and saved his life, but the impact of the bullet must have knocked him unconscious.

She examined the tear, her heart racing. The sense of vulnerability, of utter powerlessness, that had risen up inside her when she'd knelt over Lewis outside the cinema just a few nights ago shivered through her again, laced with a fierce rage.

Someone had tried to kill McCabe.

Her fingers brushed the hard butt of his gun where

it was strapped to his thigh. Jaw clenched, she dragged the Glock free of the holster, thumbed the safety and swung it, two-handed, in an arc as she looked out over the auditorium.

As abruptly as if she'd flicked a switch, sound and light and colour hit her. The place was wild with people trying to get out. The doorways were jammed, chairs overturned, the noise horrendous. Somewhere, in the midst of all that confusion, was a killer.

Ben groaned, his eyes flipped open. Memory roared back on a flood of adrenaline. He tried to roll onto his side, but his chest hurt and he couldn't move his legs. Something was pinning them. He went for the Glock, but his hand came out clean; the holster was empty. Disbelief made his head swim; then he heard West's crooning voice and realised that the weight pinning his legs was Roma. She was crouched over him, holding the Glock in a two-handed grip, levelling it at the crowd.

A flash went off. Her hand jerked.

He heard West telling her not to shoot the photographer.

"I know who to shoot and not to shoot," she retorted.

Ben turned his head and caught West's calm gaze. "Is it clear?" he asked, knowing the question was rhetorical. If West had the time to talk Roma out of shooting a reporter, their shooter was long gone.

"As day," West replied. "The lady's got the gun.

Talk her down, mate, before the police decide she's a threat.''

Ben propped himself on his elbows, wincing at the hot pain spreading across his chest. ''Drop the gun, honey. We need to get off this catwalk.''

Roma shot him a fierce look. ''What if he shoots again?''

''What if *who* shoots again? You see him out there? The place is crazy with people.''

Another flash went off. Ben turned his head in time to see the enterprising photographer run for the door, unaware that he was lucky to be alive. Ben pushed himself into a sitting position, gritting his teeth against the pain. Oh, yeah, the legend continues. He could see the headline now: Lombard Heiress Protects Bodyguard. The media had crucified him over the past week, labelling him the bodyguard lover. What was left of his reputation had just officially been shot to ribbons.

West eased onto the catwalk in a fluid movement and went down on his haunches beside Roma. In a silver-grey suit and black T-shirt, his hair caught back in some kind of antique silver clasp, he looked big and calm and exotically urbane. ''There's no one to shoot, Roma.'' Certainty laced his soft, dark drawl. ''He's gone.''

Roma eyed West solemnly. ''How do you know?''

West gently took the gun from her hands. He jerked his head toward the back of the auditorium. ''He made his shot and left. I saw him slide through the door. I tried to get to him, but there were too many people in the way. But don't worry, we'll get him. We know what he looks like now, so we can start working to identify him. And if he's prepared to expose himself to that extent to make his shot, then he isn't going to be hard to catch.''

Chapter 17

Three hours later Ben phoned down to reception to hold all calls unless they were from the Lombard family, set the phone down and peeled off his T-shirt so Carter could take a look at his chest.

Carter eyed the grapefruit-size bruise in the centre of Ben's chest, unzipped the first-aid kit he'd brought up to the suite with him and extracted a tube of ointment. "Sit down," he said, jerking his head toward the dining table. "This is going to hurt."

"Tell me about it," Ben muttered, easing down onto a chair, then stiffening as Carter began smearing ointment across the area. Carter was an excellent medic; he'd trained in hospitals and done a lot of medical work in combat situations and third world countries, but his bedside manner wasn't exactly comforting. "Ouch!"

Carter capped the ointment and put it back in his kit. He glanced around the room, blue eyes cold. "Where's Roma?"

"In the shower."

She'd been uncharacteristically quiet ever since they'd got back to the suite, and Ben was worried, but he hadn't had a chance to get her alone yet. The phone hadn't stopped ringing, and Carter and West had been with him the entire time, sticking so close he was beginning to feel caged. They hadn't said anything, but he knew what they were doing; they were acting as his personal guard, and he knew they would stay with him until they were certain he was safe. Ben hadn't argued, because he knew there was no point. If he were in their position, he would do exactly the same thing.

West prowled the length of the room, reached the open bifold doors, turned and surveyed the room, his gaze restless. Ben noted he still had his shoulder rig on. For that matter, so did Carter.

"Stop pacing, you're making me nervous."

West's gaze flashed over him. "You *should* be nervous. The guy was good with a handgun. Hit dead-centre. If he's the same shooter who did Roma's friend in Sydney, we've got a problem."

Carter extracted a couple of painkillers from a foil packet and slapped them down in front of Ben. "I'm betting it's the same guy."

So was Ben. They'd spent a good two hours with the police, giving statements, running through moti-

vations and possible suspects. West had provided a
physical description, but the identikit was inconclu-
sive. Lean, medium height, dark blond hair, in the
forty-plus age group…the description fit a huge list
of known criminals and terrorists. And that was always presupposing the hair colour was correct. The
police had taken the body armour with the bullet still
embedded in it away for analysis, along with a handgun that had been found beneath a seat, apparently
placed there by the shooter. The Luger was an un-
usual weapon, more a collector's piece than a street
gun. And finding it had filled them all with disbelief.
It was the kind of break that only happened in the
movies, but they'd had to accept that it was the
weapon that had been used against Ben, because it
had recently been discharged. The only reason they
could come up with for the shooter to leave the
weapon where it would be easily found was because
he wanted them to find it. As to *why* he would want
them to find it, no one knew.

Carter filled a glass of water and placed it by the
pain killers. "What did Gray say?"

Ben swallowed the pills, grimacing. "Not much
that's printable."

West stopped pacing. "Did you tell him Roma had
your gun?"

Ben eyed them both. They had innocent looks on
their faces, which was a difficult feat. The last time
either of them had been innocent had been when they

were in a cradle. "I didn't have to. He already knew. Some reporter beat me to it."

There was a period of silence, in which West took an inordinate interest in studying the shrubs on the terrace, and which Carter filled by examining the contents of the fridge. He came back to the table with three cans of orange juice and the remains of a cold pizza.

West dropped down into a chair and picked up a slice of the pizza. "Speaking of guns," he murmured as he settled back in his chair, "if I were you, I'd get another set of body armour. You survived one shot today, but guess who hits town in about—" he checked his watch, and whistled "—half an hour."

Blade.

Ben pulled on his T-shirt. Oh, yeah, Gray *and* Blade. Perfect.

Carter nudged the pizza carton in his direction. Ben noticed that he'd been left the scrawniest piece. There were some boundaries that even friendship didn't breach.

"You got an engagement ring?" Carter asked, apparently more interested in the dietary information on the juice can than any answer Ben might come up with. "I can go out and get one for you, if you want."

Ben eyed Carter narrowly as he snagged his piece of pizza. "I can get my own ring."

Carter and West exchanged grins, then sat back to wait.

* * *

Blade arrived first, dressed in faded jeans and a white T-shirt, long black hair sleeked back in a ponytail, dark eyes fierce. He'd used his own private helicopter, landing on the pad on the roof of the hotel. "What happened?" he snapped, when Ben opened the door. "Where's Roma?"

Roma cocked her head at the sound of Blade's voice, her heart filling with a mixture of delight and resignation as she pulled on jeans and a soft cotton checked shirt and braced herself to walk out into the lounge.

She'd spent the last hour piecing herself together after the shooting and the seemingly endless time spent sitting in a police interview room at Auckland Central, watching Ben treat the fact that he'd been shot with the same kind of distance the police did. It wasn't a distance Roma was very good at holding on to, but she'd had to. There had been a lot of ground to cover between the Sydney shooting and this one, and Ben had been shut off from her, not only by the demands of the investigation, but by West and Carter, who'd closed ranks around him. Even when they'd returned to the hotel, West and Carter had made it clear who they were protecting, and from what. Understanding that she wasn't personally to blame for the threat didn't help much. The threat existed. And so long as she was close to Ben, he was in danger.

Blade strode up to Roma, gripped her arms, stared into her eyes. "You all right, baby?"

"I'm—"

He pulled her into a hug, not waiting for an answer. "We'll get the bastard," he stated coldly.

Blade's wife, Anna, handed him the baby to hold and hugged Roma. "At least he's a bad shot. Chances are he'll be sloppy in other ways."

Gray arrived with Samantha and their twins in tow. Suddenly the room was overflowing with people, and this was only the beginning. The entire family was due to arrive for the ball that evening.

Gray hugged her, set her away from him and gave her a piercing look. "How in hell did you get McCabe's gun?"

Blade's head came up. "She got Ben's gun?"

Roma switched her attention to Blade, frowning. The whole lot of them had missed the point, just as they had with Lewis. They were all focused on her, but it was Ben who'd been shot.

Blade grinned. "Did you shoot him, baby?" he crooned. "Please tell me you shot him."

Gray eyed her with something between frustration and amusement. "She didn't get the bad guy, but she drew a bead on the damn reporter. You can read about it in the paper tomorrow."

Gray's wife, Sam, straightened from unstrapping the twins from their double stroller and sent Blade a reproving look. "Don't look so happy, Blade. If she'd shot the reporter, she'd have to go to prison, and then we'd have to break her out."

Sam enveloped Roma in a hug. The twins stag-

gered forward and wrapped their plump little arms
around her legs and gave her baby hugs, begging to
be picked up. Roma went down on her haunches,
happy to concentrate on her niece and nephew and
their uncomplicated needs while Ben fielded a barrage of questions from her family. She hugged the
twins close, breathing in their sweet baby scents and
enjoying their wriggling, squirming little bodies, the
sloppy kisses they planted on her cheeks.

Minutes later her cousin Cullen walked in, followed by his wife, Rachel, and their two children,
Emma and Jake Junior, who had been predictably
nicknamed JJ. Cullen's grey eyes fixed on her, cool
and considering. He walked up to her and gave her
a hug. Of all the members of the family, he was the
most enigmatic. All the Lombard men were take-
charge kind of men. Blade was a handful in any situation you cared to name, Gray was just flat-out
dominant, but Cullen had a gentleness to him completely at odds with his big warrior's body. Not that
most people ever got past the wintry-grey shield of
his gaze to that core of gentleness.

The twins were still hanging on to her legs, and
Emma and Jake Junior were clustered around her,
when Elsa McCabe arrived, with Bunny in tow,
swelling the numbers in the suite even further.

Ben made introductions around the room, then
submitted to having his T-shirt pulled up while both
Elsa and Bunny examined his chest. Elsa was pale,
her expression controlled, but it was Bunny who held

Roma's attention. The little girl stayed close to Ben, big eyes dark and solemn.

JJ tugged at her sleeve and shoved a book at her, wanting a story, and Roma dragged her gaze away from the picture of Ben trying to explain to his mother and daughter just how he'd come to get shot.

She made it to a couch, weighted down with slow-moving toddlers. The twins both tried to plop their soft little rumps on her lap. Emma shook her head in exasperation, sat down and heaved one of the twins onto her lap, exclaiming loudly at the weight. Little Nathaniel, the older of Gray and Sam's twins by ten minutes, stared at Emma, mesmerised, and stuck his thumb in his mouth.

JJ wiggled in beside her and patted the book. "Read," he said happily.

Roma opened the book and began to read. After a few minutes Emma wriggled out from beneath Nathaniel and wandered over to watch Anna feed her baby, and Bunny McCabe took Emma's place on the couch, smiling shyly as she hefted Nathaniel onto her lap and cuddled him close.

The persistent, distant buzz of a cell phone sounded, almost lost in the torrent of noise filling the suite. When it finally registered that it was her phone, Roma eased herself free of children, walked into her room and answered the call. At first she couldn't quite hear what the caller was saying; then a few words registered.

Roma went still inside. "Who are you?"

"Someone you know, yet don't know."

Her jaw squared, and she repeated her question.

There was a pause. "I can't see you now, you've gone into your room, but I could see you before…with the children, your family. McCabe." The last was uttered with a flatness that sent a cold shock of awareness through her.

Her hand tightened on the phone. "You shot Ben."

"I also sent you the photos. And I was in Sydney not long ago. Your friend Lewis Harrington's recovering well. I know. I checked on him."

"Why are you doing this?" she demanded fiercely. *"Leave us alone."*

"Don't let McCabe close to you again."

The phone went dead as the call was terminated.

Michael Linden slipped his cell phone into his overnight case, snapped it closed and straightened. It was time to leave. The Lombard men would move on him fast once they realised he was so close. Gray and Blade were cold, efficient bastards, and they were dogged. They'd hunted Harper down, even though it had taken years. And he'd seen Cullen Logan in the suite. Logan had been out of the loop for a while, but Linden didn't underestimate him, just as he didn't underestimate McCabe, West or Rawlings. He'd made it his business to find out everything he could about their respective careers and their lives, unwilling, out of sheer habit, to let any detail slip.

But he'd also been fascinated by the men who saw him as prey. They'd worked together for years in the SAS; they were a tightly woven team—as near as damn it to the legendary pagoda squads that had operated out of Britain years ago that it didn't make any difference.

And now they were now hunting him.

A hot thrill shot up Linden's spine. He grinned coldly. Not that they had a hope in hell of catching him…unless he chose to let them.

He picked up his overnighter and the photographer's case that held his weapons, cast his eye over the hotel room one more time, then walked calmly to the door, stopping to check his appearance in the mirror. With his sober tie and lightweight jacket, he looked smooth, urbane, a businessman on a trip—if it hadn't been for the edgy glitter of excitement in his eyes.

He stared at himself, riveted, feeling that disorienting shifting sensation inside. He looked alive in a way he hadn't for the past year. There was nothing about his appearance that suggested he would be dead in a month.

Roma pulled her purse out of her holdall, searched through the contents and pulled out credit cards and all the cash. Her fingers shook so much that the cards scattered on the floor. Taking a calming breath, she methodically picked them up, folded the bills around the cards, making a tight bundle, and slipped it all into the front pocket of her jeans. Next she found her passport and slipped that into her back pocket. She couldn't take the holdall, or even the purse. She couldn't even afford to carry any items of clothing with her, or wear a jacket. If she looked as though she was going somewhere, she was more likely to be noticed and stopped, and once her family and Ben knew what she was going to do, she wouldn't get another chance; they would watch her every second.

With hands that were still annoyingly unsteady, she extracted the Sig from the sweatshirt she'd wrapped it in, checked the safety, then slid it beneath the waistband of her jeans in the small of her back. The metal was cold against her skin, and the gun sat uncomfortably, the shape and weight awkward, but there was no other solution.

She resettled her shirt over the gun, turned to the side and examined the effect in the mirror. The fall of the loose shirt hid the gun well enough that she could walk out of the suite with it, and that was all she needed.

She took another moment to study herself in the mirror. She was breathing too fast, and her face was pale, but otherwise she looked remarkably composed, her expression as blank as her mind. Later on, she would have time to feel, but she couldn't allow herself the luxury of emotion yet.

Her hair was loose. She would have to change that. Rummaging through a drawer, she found a red baseball cap and stuffed it in her back pocket, where the bulge was hidden by the fall of her shirt. When she got free of the suite, she would twist her hair into a knot and stuff it beneath the cap.

Taking a deep breath, she opened the door and stepped out into the lounge.

The sudden blast of noise was overpowering, battering her senses after the calm of her room. The television was on in the corner. Bunny, Emma, Jake and the twins were camped around it amid a jumble of toys, watching a cartoon. Anna was changing her baby in a corner and chatting with Jack and Millie, who must have arrived while Roma was in her room. Jack was a long-time employee and friend of the family. Over the years, he'd *become* family. Someone was clattering in the kitchen; the deliciously savoury scent of onions frying permeated the air. Most of the men were camped around the dining table or hanging out in the kitchen, their voices a rumble of sound as they presumably went over every aspect of the shootings.

A fight broke out in front of the television as the twins tussled over a ragged teddy bear, followed by a howl of outrage as JJ discovered that the two toddlers had filched his favourite toy. Millie and Jack's baby, who had been sound asleep in a carry cot, woke up and began crying, his high-pitched wails adding to the cacophony of sound. The suite erupted into chaos as parents leapt to their feet and tried to pacify their children.

Blankly, Roma turned away from the sheer wonderful normality of the scene. She loved her family, the noise and confusion, the fights and the laughter, the sometimes smothering closeness that enveloped every member, whether a blood relation or not, in a blanket of love and warmth. They fought and argued and teased each other, but Lombards loved hard. Her family would hold her close, but she wouldn't allow any of them to put themselves at risk, and especially not now, with the suite filled with children and babies. That was the second reason she had to leave. The first reason was Ben. He would keep her with him, regardless of the danger, and she wouldn't, *couldn't,* lose him in that way.

She'd thought it through, but no matter how she approached the problem, the most effective solution was always the same. If she removed herself from Ben, she removed the immediate danger. It wasn't a complete answer, because she couldn't remain in hiding forever, but she would take that hurdle when she got to it.

As soon as she was free of the building, she would phone Gray and warn him that the suite was under surveillance.

As she grasped the handle of the door, the buzzer sounded, shocking her into immobility.

"Get the door, Roma!" Blade yelled.

She flinched, then mechanically opened the door, standing aside as Sadie Carson barrelled in. Tony Fa'alau followed at a more sedate pace, courtesy of his limp.

''Heard you had some trouble today, girl,'' Sadie said, reaching up and pecking her on the cheek. ''Came to give you a hand.''

Tony greeted her in his usual gentle manner, then there was a shout of *''Sadie''*, and Blade walked over, scooped Sadie up in a bear hug and swung her around. ''How's my girl?'' he teased.

Sadie blushed. ''Put me down, you devil. We can't have any more of this nonsense. I'm a married woman now.'' She grinned when Blade set her down, and slotted herself in the curve of her new husband's arm. ''We eloped,'' she said happily. ''Didn't want any fuss and bother.''

The noise level went crazy as Sadie and Tony were surrounded and congratulated. One of the babies woke up and howled with displeasure at having his nap interrupted, and Nathaniel took advantage of the momentary lapse in supervision and clambered onto the coffee table, knocking a bag filled with baby bottles and fresh diapers onto the floor, and crowing in happy delight at the accomplishment.

In the midst of all the confusion, Roma slipped from the room and closed the door gently behind her, heart pounding as she walked toward the lift. The security monitors were all on in the suite; if anyone glanced in their general direction, they would see her leaving.

When she reached the lift, she pressed the button to open the doors and found she had to wait; the security people who'd escorted Sadie and Tony to the suite had just used the lift to return to their sta-

tion. Seconds felt like minutes as she stood staring
at the polished stainless-steel doors, willing them to
open, aware of the security camera boring into her
back.

Finally the light glowed, indicating that the lift
was on its way back up. When the doors slid open,
Roma stepped in, jabbed the button to close the doors
and held her breath as the lift began to descend. The
lift camera was small, but this one caught her face-
on. With any luck the security people monitoring the
lift wouldn't question the fact that she was unaccom-
panied until it was too late. She didn't doubt that they
would question why she was wandering around the
hotel on her own—McCabe was too efficient not to
have covered that base—but it was hardly a crisis
situation. She was still in the centre of the security
net, watched and protected; there wouldn't be cause
for alarm until she was observed leaving the secured
area.

The second she left the building all hell would
break loose, but she would be free and clear before
they had time to react.

With jerky movements, she rearranged her hair,
winding it into a knot, jamming the cap over top and
tucking loose strands beneath it. She pulled the bill
of the cap down and examined the effect in the mirror. She couldn't change her face, but this way people would look twice—used to seeing her with her
hair loose or wound up in an elegant knot. The cap
was also an eye-catching red; if anyone looked at her
they would notice the cap before anything else, and

the bill cast her eyes into shadow, adding another layer of deception. As disguises went, it wasn't much, but all she needed were those few seconds of hesitation.

The doors slid open. Roma stepped out and turned sharply right, walking quickly toward the rear of the hotel and the car park. She wasn't leaving by the front. If the gunman had been able to see into the lounge of the suite, that meant he was in one of the buildings across the road from the main hotel entrance.

She didn't fool herself that Ben wouldn't be able to track her movements at the rear of the hotel; the security system incorporated a series of video cameras in all the major traffic areas. She would be observed until she left the car park.

The glass doors to the car park parted as she approached, and one of the hotel security staff stepped through. A shock of adrenaline went through her as he glanced at her, gaze moving across her face and locking on the cap.

Roma walked past him, heart racing, her breath impeded. When she glanced back over her shoulder he was still watching her, his radio out.

Adrenaline pumped again, but she held herself to a sedate walk. If she looked as if she were hurrying, he would come after her. Seconds later she walked down the exit ramp, took a right turn, then a left, and joined the bustling crowds of shoppers and office workers inhabiting central Auckland.

* * *

Ben searched the suite, then slammed the palm of his hand on the door of Roma's room. She was gone. He snapped out an order for someone to ring down to security, then jerked the front door open and headed for the lift. Carter, West, Blade and Gray piled in with him.

All the way down, he cursed himself. He should have known she was up to something; he should have watched her, kept her by his side, but he'd made the basic mistake of letting her have her space while her family was there, and he hadn't wanted her in on the discussion about how they were going to hunt down the guy who was stalking her. The last time he'd looked, she'd been cuddling babies.

She'd been too quiet, too subdued. God only knew what had been going through her head. She'd hated the fact that he'd been shot, but she'd stopped fussing a while ago. He would take note of that in future, he thought grimly; if she was quiet, that meant all hell was about to break loose.

The doors slid open. Ben didn't bother to stop at reception but headed straight for the street. The late-afternoon sun hit his eyes, making him squint as he swept the bustling scene. Heat radiated from the pavement, shimmered off bitumen. Rush-hour traffic was gridlocked at the lights, and everywhere he looked there were holiday-makers, shoppers and office workers walking to their cars or the buses, university students strolling from their last lecture of the day.

West joined him. "Security said she walked out

through the car park. Guess she was too quick for them.''

"She was too quick for all of us.''

Seconds later Carter appeared, his face grim. "What do we do now?''

Ben surveyed the busy street, automatically studying people, cars, his mind working over everything that had happened and coming up with a frustrating blank. He had no idea where she had gone. "We comb this damn city until we find her.''

And he *would* find her. She was in danger, and it was his fault. He hadn't paid enough attention. He'd forgotten who she was, the events that had moulded her character. West had reminded him at the fashion show when he'd coaxed Roma to give up Ben's gun. He had warned him that she was a Lombard, and that she had a gun in her hand, but he'd continued to disregard her for the classic male reason: because she was female. But she'd acted cool under fire twice now in a matter of days, putting her own personal safety at risk to protect those she cared for. Male or female, it made no difference; she was a damn gunslinger, just like her brothers. Now she'd decided to strike out on her own, and his gut twisted with dread.

The gunman was targeting men who were close to Roma, but they only had a sample base of two incidents; the pattern could change without notice. She'd removed herself not only to keep him safe, but to protect everyone she loved. When her family had arrived with all the babies and small children, she must have been horrified at the possibilities.

She'd picked her time and slipped out amid the chaos of all the arrivals. Ben had been only minutes behind her, but he might as well have been days late; the trail was already cold.

Blade joined them on the pavement. "I checked the car park and rear of the building. No sign of her there." He shook his head and echoed Ben's sentiment. "I should have known she was up to something. She was too damn quiet."

Gray arrived seconds later. He flipped his cell phone closed and slipped it into his pocket. "I've phoned the taxi companies. They're checking on fares."

Ben shook his head. "She wouldn't have taken a taxi. Would you have?"

Gray scanned the street, fixed on the busy bus stop in the distance. He looked thoughtful. "No. She would have walked, maybe caught a bus if there was one leaving straight away." His gaze swung back to Ben, the tension that had shimmered, unacknowledged, between them ever since Gray had stepped into the suite finally out in the open. "We know this guy's shooting anyone who gets too close to Roma. The question is," he murmured coldly, "just how close did you get?"

Blade stepped forward, black eyes glittering. Gray's hand clamped his arm, restraining him.

Ben met Gray's gaze, then Blade's. When he replied, his voice was equally cold. "Close enough to know she's mine."

Chapter 18

Gray's cell phone rang, breaking the tension. Seconds later, the call was terminated.

"That was Roma," he said tersely. "The son of a bitch called her. Somehow he got hold of her number." He looked up at the hotel opposite, his gaze bleak. "She said he could see her, that he was watching. He described what was happening in the suite."

Minutes later they were standing in a hotel room directly across from the Lombard suite.

The tripod was still set up at the window, the camera trained on the terrace of the Lombard suite. The bed was neatly made, although it was wrinkled, as if someone had lain down on it after it had been made. There were toiletries left in the bathroom and clothes neatly folded in the drawers. The room was eerily complete, as if the occupant had just stepped out for a few minutes. There were no signs that it had been abandoned in a hurry.

"Cocky," Blade said grimly. "Or crazy. He chose the most obvious room."

Ben took in the details, all his senses condensing into cold alertness. "Something doesn't fit," he said slowly. "This guy's a professional. He wouldn't have stayed in this room. He would have used it strictly for surveillance and stayed somewhere else. And why has he left everything behind, when he knows he's not coming back?"

He took a pen from his pocket, lifted the lid of a briefcase which was sitting on the bureau beside the television, careful not to touch anything before the cops had a chance to dust the room for prints. He studied the contents. A passport sat neatly on top of a stack of photos, the first of which was a portrait of Roma taken when she was younger, her hair in a plait. Ben's jaw tightened. He used the pen to flip the document open. The colour snapshot showed a man with blond hair, a tanned face, his features aquiline, eyes a pale, colourless grey. According to the passport details, his name was Michael Linden. He was fifty-two years of age, but he looked younger, his face lean and firmly contoured, as if he kept himself in good physical condition.

Something cold and hard settled in his gut. He didn't know the man—he was a stranger—but the emerging personality was familiar. Oh, yeah, he'd met his kind before, seen those dead eyes. He was willing to bet the guy was a mercenary, or a hired gun of some type, with an added kink to his character: he was stalking a woman young enough to be his daughter. "The bastard's playing some kind of game," he said flatly. "This whole room is staged. He wanted us to find this stuff. And he wants us to know who he is."

West looked at the passport photo. "That's the guy who shot you," he murmured. "Be interesting to see if his identity is legit."

Gray's phone rang again. When he terminated the call, his expression was curiously blank.

Blade's head came up, his dark eyes sharp. "What is it?"

"I got our people to run the description of the handgun the shooter used through our data base. They came up with a match. The gun is the same make and model as the one that killed Jake's fiancée nine years ago. We'll have to wait for the analysis on the bullet, but I'm betting we've hit pay dirt. After all these years we've finally found the hit man Harper contracted to execute Jake."

The wind gusted, tugging strands of Roma's hair from beneath her baseball cap as she walked down the street toward her motel. Automatically, she adjusted the grip on the bag of groceries she was carrying, her gaze skimming the street, noting people and cars.

It was hot, the sky leaden with dark, sulphurous clouds, the air charged with ozone and heavy with the promise of rain. Her skin prickled uncomfortably beneath the cheap, oversize shirt she'd bought, but comfort was secondary. The shirt was like a dozen others she'd seen at the mall where she'd done her shopping. It flapped around her thighs, disguising her figure so that she could be taken for any one of the androgynous teenagers hanging out at the mall, and easily covering the gun slipped into the small of her back. The cap added to the effect, hiding her hair and shading her face, making her even more anonymous.

A low rumble had her glancing at the sky. Several large droplets of rain plopped down, hitting the dusty pavement in front of her. Water splashed off the bill of her cap, but she couldn't work up the energy to care if she got wet or stayed dry. The sky had been grumbling, threatening for the past half hour, with no result except that the day had gotten hotter and even more humid, resembling nothing so much as a steam bath.

When she reached her unit, she slipped the key out of her jeans pocket and inserted it in the lock. She'd been here three days now, and her situation was still unresolved. She'd rung Gray as soon as she'd gotten the room, and explained what she was doing and why. He'd gone crazy. She'd listened for a few seconds, then terminated the call and turned off her cell phone. She didn't want Gray or Ben trying to ring her or track her down, and she didn't want the gunman ringing her. She went cold every time she considered how he'd managed to get her number. He'd either snooped through the private records of one of the few people who had her number, or he'd gotten close enough to her to get it. If that was the case, he would have had to take her phone from her holdall, note the number, then replace the phone, all without her or any of the security people around her noticing.

In a few days, when most of the fuss had died down, she would take a bus to another city, go to the international terminal, wait until it was almost time to board, then buy a ticket from the airline counter for a flight to Sydney. Her name wouldn't appear on the passenger manifest until the plane was practically in the air. It would be too late for her brothers, or Ben, to catch up with her. Too late for Ben to try to protect her and, in doing so, put himself in danger.

Briefly she relived the moment when he'd been hit in the chest, and a shudder moved through her as she pushed open her door and stepped inside.

She'd avoided thinking about Ben, and for the first few hours after she'd left the hotel, she'd almost succeeded. Finding the motel had been her first priority. That hadn't been difficult. She'd simply ridden buses for a couple of hours, until she'd become tired and hungry; then she'd gotten off and walked until she'd seen a motel sign.

Her unit was small, dark, bordering on tacky, with the bare essentials of a double bed, a couple of easy chairs grouped around a television and a cheap dining set next to the kitchenette. After she'd checked in, paying cash, she'd walked to the nearest shopping centre and bought some basic groceries, remembering to include toothpaste and a toothbrush, and a comb for her hair. She'd barely noticed what she'd put in her trolley, let alone cared. She'd been numb, although that had soon changed.

The days were bad enough, because she was at loose ends, yet too wound up to read or to watch television, but the nights were worse. At night she ached for Ben. The temptation to ring him and simply hear his voice gnawed at her, at times so great that she considered throwing her phone away, because if she heard his voice, she would break and probably beg him to come and get her.

She shifted the grocery bag onto her hip as she closed the door and slipped the key back into her pocket. She was going to have to buy more clothes, another pair of jeans, a couple of T-shirts, perhaps risk using her cash card again. This time she'd simply bought the minimum: food and underwear.

When she got home…

Dully, she considered flying home, but the thought of leaving the city where Ben lived, let alone the country, was wrenching. At least here she was physically close to him, even if she couldn't be with him. When she did get home, her options were limited. She would have to live under heavy security until the situation was resolved.

The motel unit was dim inside, the temperature slightly cooler than outside, because she'd left all the curtains drawn when she went shopping. A subtle difference in the air, a sense of not being alone, made Roma freeze in the act of putting on the chain. Her nape tightened, all the fine hairs lifting as she let the chain drop and turned, using the bag of groceries to shield the movement of her arm as she reached back and groped for the Sig.

Ben was sitting sprawled in one of the easy chairs near the television, blue eyes glittering in the shadows as he watched her.

The breath jerked from her lungs, and her knees turned to jelly. For a moment she thought she might have conjured him up because she wanted him so much, but he wasn't an illusion. It was Ben; he was here.

She leaned back against the door, the gun digging into her spine, as she hungrily soaked in all the details of his appearance. He was wearing a white T-shirt and a pair of faded jeans, and he looked wonderful. Then reality intruded. If Ben could find her, then the person stalking her could, too.

Her attempts at hiding hadn't been sophisticated; she'd simply opted for cheap accommodation because it was easier for her to be anonymous in a down market area, and she'd tried to keep a low profile. Obviously it hadn't worked.

"Were you going to contact me?" His voice reflected a mild interest in her answer as he eased to his feet and covered the distance between them, but she wasn't fooled. He looked big and remote and dangerous. The very air sizzled with tension.

"When I got home I would have rung you."

He was still for a moment; then he took the bag of groceries from her, strolled to the kitchenette and dumped the bag on the bench.

Roma wanted to walk up to him, wrap her arms around his waist and bury her face against his back, but his very restraint stopped her. "How did you find me?"

Instead of putting groceries away, as she expected, he opened up her fridge and began placing the few meagre items in with the things she'd bought.

"None of the rental car agencies turned up any evidence that you'd obtained a car, so I worked on the assumption that you were still in the general area. You used a cash card at the local mall yesterday, which narrowed the search. I canvassed all the lower priced hotels and motels, because I knew you wouldn't risk staying at any of the more expensive ones in case you were recognised. Only problem is, you're a distinctive-looking woman. People remember you—especially men. The guy at the front desk nailed you instantly."

Roma straightened away from the door, watching blankly as he finished cleaning out the fridge and began inspecting her cupboards. "You know why I left."

He gathered up the groceries and put the bag on the dining table. It was then that she noticed he'd already packed what meagre possessions she had; they were stacked in a small pile on the table. He was ready to leave, and he was taking her with him.

Briefly she considered running. There was nothing there she couldn't leave behind. She was carrying her credit cards, passport and gun on her against just such an eventuality. She'd even been sleeping in her clothes, the gun under her pillow, because she needed everything within reach if she had to move quickly. But one look at McCabe told her she wouldn't get far.

"I know why you thought you had to leave," he amended as he moved to the window beside her and shifted the curtain just enough to see outside. "But you had to know I'd come after you."

"So what now?" she demanded. "What if he's watching?"

"I'm not leaving you to face this alone, so get used to that fact."

Roma's jaw tightened. "You are so hard-headed, McCabe, you drive me crazy. I love you. I *left* for you, and it wasn't easy. Now you're ruining everything. What about Bunny?"

His gaze swept her. "She's safe," he said absently. "My mother's taking care of her, and Gray's taking care of them. He chartered a flight and sent everyone who's not needed to Sydney. You just said you loved me.'' He let the curtain drop, then reached over and pulled the cap off her hair so that it cascaded around her shoulders. "I hate this cap." He tossed it aside and stepped closer, tangling his fingers in her hair. "Don't wear one again."

She closed her eyes against the sensation of his fingers gently combing through her hair. "You're a control freak, McCabe."

"I know, and now you're going to wear baseball caps every day." His breath stirred against her forehead. "And you say I drive *you* crazy? When you walked out of that suite, you took ten years off my life." He cupped her face. "The guy who's stalking you isn't on the level. He keeps leaving us clues. We found ammunition in his room that matched the bullet that was taken out of Lewis Harrington's shoulder. The markings on the bullet that was dug out of my body armour are a perfect match for the bullet that killed your brother's fiancée nine years ago. You think this guy only shoots men? Think again. One of the names he uses is Michael Linden, and he's a contract killer—a hit man—and he's on Interpol's Most Wanted list. His kill list is longer than my arm, and those are only the known kills. The only reason we're getting close to him is because he's letting us. He's the hit man who killed your brother, honey. You aren't safe. I found you, which means he's one step behind, because I know for a fact that the canny bastard's been following me."

"He killed Jake?" She felt oddly distant, as if the room and everything in it were receding.

"I'm sorry," Ben said roughly. "But I meant to shock you. You can't fight this one alone, and I'm not going to let you."

She found herself ushered toward a chair, Mc-Cabe's arm around her waist. He sat her down, squatted beside her and coaxed her head between her legs.

"Linden's wanted by so many people, you wouldn't believe it. Gray and Blade are going crazy trying to keep a lid on what's happened. The media are camped on the doorstep of the hotel."

She lifted her head, still feeling disoriented. "So what do we do next?"

In her mind, the man who'd killed Jake wasn't just a person with a gun, he was an unstoppable monster. He'd haunted her dreams for years, and now he was back, shadowy and elusive and lethal.

"We give him what he wants. A hunt." Ben rose and collected her possessions from the table, then ushered her to the door, once more lifting the curtain and checking outside before he pushed the door open. "First we let Linden see us together. You're going to have a ring on your finger. My ring. When he realises you're engaged to me, he'll go crazy. After that we head for the country for the weekend. Cullen's put his hunting lodge at our disposal, which will put Linden in unfamiliar territory. All we have to do is wait for him to make a mistake."

"But how can you guarantee he'll follow? If he's comfortable in the city, won't he just wait until we come back?"

"He'll follow. He's gone to a lot of effort to get

our attention. He won't drop the ball now. Interpol
sent through a piece of information yesterday that
clarifies why he's gone off the deep end, and what
he actually wants. Linden's dying of cancer, and he
wants us to hunt him. He's looking for an execution.''

When they reached the Lombard Hotel, Ben took
her to an unfamiliar suite on the other side of the
building. Carter and West accompanied them as far
as the door, then left them to their privacy; they were
occupying the suite next door.

Roma deposited her perishables in the fridge.

Ben placed a black gear bag on the dining table,
unzipped it and began transferring electronic gear
into it from the table. ''Grab a shower and get
changed, and when you're ready, we'll go shopping
for a ring. Blade's organized the publicity for this,
so it's going to be ritzy.''

Roma closed the fridge door and asked the question that had been eating at her all the way there.
''Have you thought about what happens if you get
killed trying to trap this guy? What will happen to
Bunny?''

He picked up an unfamiliar handgun, ejected the
empty clip, then began slotting in shells from a box
of ammunition. ''I've lived with that level of risk for
years—every time I went on an SAS mission. And
so has my family.'' His gaze was cold, uncompromising. ''The time to get Linden is now. He's vulnerable because he wants you, but sooner or later that

vulnerability is going to tick him off. He's going to decide that shooting the guys you go out with isn't enough. He's going to get jealous of anyone you spend time with. Eventually he'll tip right over the edge and decide that if he can't have you, no one can. And that's when you become a target." He slid the clip home and calmly put the gun down on the table before picking up a second handgun and ejecting the empty clip. "That's not going to happen."

Ben didn't add his own private fear: that Roma was very probably the ultimate target anyway. He didn't know how unbalanced Linden was, with his own death approaching, but the man might very well reach a point in his reasoning where he decided that if he was going to die, then Roma should die with him.

"Does anything ever stop you, McCabe?"

"Yeah." A smile tugged at the corner of his mouth. "She's about five foot five, mouthy, and a whole lot of trouble. Go and have that shower before I decide to get in with you. You may not have been counting, but I have, and it's been three days. The only reason I haven't kissed you is because if I do, we won't be going anywhere for a while."

A little shudder ran through her. "You've been counting days? I've been counting nights."

Ben went utterly still. He set the gun down. The click as metal connected with wood was loud in the thick silence of the room. He started toward her, peeling off his T-shirt and discarding it as he walked. His gaze locked on hers. "You are going to kill me."

She wound her arms around his neck and lifted her mouth to his, relieved that he'd put the situation with Linden aside, that he was hers, even if it was only for a short time. "Bet on it."

The exclusive jeweller housed in the Lombard retail complex was jammed with people, most of them media hounds.

Roma stared at the tray of rings, barely able to concentrate, let alone focus. Her whole body was still tingling and throbbing from the hour she and McCabe had spent in the shower, and added to that, she still hadn't adjusted to the shock of learning just who the gunman was.

"That one." Ben picked the ring off the bed of midnight velvet and slipped it on her finger. The fit was slightly loose, but it was snug enough to stay on.

The stone was a huge, tawny diamond hewn from the Argyll mines in Western Australia and set in white gold. There was no price tag, but then, Roma hadn't expected to see one.

"Yeah, I know," Ben said. He lifted her fingers to his mouth and kissed the ring. "You wanted a skull ring like the Phantom's, so you can punch Linden's lights out with it. So do I, but this'll just have to do in the meantime."

Some of the stiffness left her spine. She smiled, feeling teary-eyed at the fact that she had an engagement ring, yet no engagement, and that McCabe was trying to cheer her up with a ridiculous kid fantasy. "You wanted a Phantom ring?"

"Always."

He glanced at the jeweller, a gaunt man, who looked more like an undertaker than a man who spent his days shaping exquisite fantasies in precious metals and gems. "We'll take it."

Ben handed over his card and pulled her into his arms. "I'm going to kiss you now," he murmured. "Try to look enthusiastic."

"I know the script."

His mouth grazed hers, meltingly soft, then more firmly, until he parted her lips and stroked her tongue with his. Her eyes drifting closed, she rose up on her toes, arms curling around his neck as he kissed her more deeply.

The background murmur of conversation, the hot flash of cameras, faded. When Ben finally lifted his mouth, the silence was broken by a burst of applause.

"That should do it," he said calmly, and slid his arm around her waist as Carter and West forged a path to the door.

Chapter 19

The road wound endlessly through low hills, sleek with grass, then began to climb, precipitously one-laned and slippery with mud. The terrain changed, became harsher, steeper. Grey, lichen-rough igneous rock protruded where the wind had stripped the hillsides bare of all but a meagre covering of soil and scrubby, tough vegetation. The gentler land below supported cattle and horses; these hills were strictly sheep and goat country.

The road narrowed again, to little more than a walking track. Ben braked, unclipped his seat belt, climbed out and made a swift circuit of the truck, locking the hubs into position for four-wheel drive. When he put the truck in motion again, Roma had to hang on as they climbed. She could see the hut ahead; it was situated at the head of a broad meadow, the sides of which plummeted hundreds of feet to a thick belt of native bush below. The approach was open, with no cover. There was nowhere for Linden to set up a sniping position other than in the precipitous country behind, and to get there, he would have to pass by the hut.

The high country, on the other hand, was nothing but cover. It loomed, broodingly dark, densely cloaked in subtropical rain forest, plunging to the rocky coastland on the other side.

The Jeep skidded and wallowed along the wheel ruts that led to the hut. As Ben drew up, close to the door, it began to rain. A warm, steady downpour that greyed out the surrounding country.

"Welcome to Northland," he said dryly. "We'll need to air out the hut and light the fire. Cullen says it hasn't been used for a couple of months, so it'll be damp."

Ben reached into the back seat and handed her a raincoat, then began unloading gear. Roma awkwardly pulled on the oversize oilskin, grabbed a box of groceries and squelched across the strip of soggy grass to the hut.

It was dark inside and smelled of damp and smoke and pine timber. There were two rooms, a kitchen/dining area and the main room, which boasted a pot-bellied stove, a built-in double bed, which also served as a couch, against one wall, and a rack of four bunks on the opposite wall.

Roma opened all the windows, letting air circulate. Ben carried in an armload of wood, which he added to the partially filled box beside the pot-belly, and immediately set about lighting a fire. With the fat little stove crackling, the hut took on a cosier aspect.

He rose to his feet and dusted his hands off on his jeans. "It's primitive, but everything's here. There's an outside shower, and a chemical toilet in the lean-to. I'm just going to have a walk around and install a couple of early warning systems. Will you be all right?"

"Fine."

"Just yell if you need me, okay?"

He hitched a rucksack over one shoulder. Roma had watched him pack it and knew he had laser alarms, radios, night-vision gear and other technical gadgets she could only guess at, along with a supply of batteries and a battery charger that could run off the truck if needed. She watched him stride down the hill, and the apprehension she'd held at bay seeped back. The police and Interpol had set up a broad network of operations to catch Linden, and Blade, Gray, Cullen, West and Carter formed a protective net around the hut, just in case Linden eluded capture. They were all out there now, moving into position, but even so, she couldn't help worrying. Linden had been operating in the shadows for years, a methodical, unseen enemy used to evading capture; it was hard to believe that he could be stopped that easily.

She began unloading groceries into the cupboard and the meat safe, which was simply a cupboard jutting out from the hut wall, the wire gauze lining allowing the cooling breeze to circulate through it, at the same time keeping out animals and insects. Ben had bought a lot of dried and tinned food, which was just as well, because there was no electricity and therefore no refrigerator. All the cooking was done on a stainless-steel gas cooker, which was set up on the crude wooden bench. Water was supplied by a header tank, which stood on an elevated platform next to the hut. The header tank also supplied the shower.

Minutes later the rain stopped and the sun came out. Birds called raucously, and there was an insistent hum of insects. The scents were lush and primitive: wet earth, the dark, resinous tang of the bush, the steamy aftermath of the rain intensifying everything.

Roma strolled outside and examined the tin lean-to that held the toilet, and the rough wooden stall and slatted platform that comprised the outside shower, enjoying the sun on her skin and the refreshing breeze. She refused to look at the brooding bush-clad hills or dwell on the fact that even now she was probably under surveillance by her family, the police, Interpol and God only knew who else. She wouldn't put it past her Aunt Sophie to be up in those hills somewhere. She hated to miss out on any of the action.

She found a plastic bucket on a hook beside the

header tank, filled the bucket with water and lugged it inside. The hut was neat and tidy, but everything was coated in a layer of grime, the windows festooned with cobwebs. She dragged the mattresses outside to air in the sun, leaned them against the side of the hut and propped them up off the damp ground with an assortment of boxes and tins she found in the lean-to.

She used the broom propped behind the door to take down all the cobwebs and sweep the place out; then she searched through the cupboard under the bench and found a scrubbing brush and a selection of cleaning materials, and set to scrubbing the bench and the small built-in dining table and settles. When those were clean, she started on the windows, happy to concentrate on doing rather than thinking.

When Ben walked in the door, the hut was fresh and aired, the mattresses back on the bunks, and there was a casserole bubbling on top of the pot-belly. It was getting dark, the long extended twilight finally fading into a deep, midnight-blue sky, so she'd lit the lantern she'd found in a cupboard and placed it on the bench where she was making damper.

He'd taken off his shirt, which hung wet and limp over one bronzed shoulder, and the rucksack dangled from his fingers. In the dim golden light, his eyes were shadowed, the bold lines of cheekbone and jaw starkly delineated.

"Something smells good."

''Steak casserole. I thought I'd better use the fresh ingredients. The meat will stay cool in the safe, but it won't keep long in this weather.''

He eased off his boots and placed them just inside the door, hung the rucksack up on a peg that was hammered into the wall and padded over to the pot-belly.

She dipped her hands into a bucket of water, washed the dough from them, then dried them on a tea towel. When she set the pan of damper on top of the pot-belly to cook, Ben glanced at her left hand.

''Where's the ring?''

She met his gaze briefly, then walked back to the bench to clean up the floury mess she'd made. ''I took it off. The engagement's just a publicity stunt to catch Linden, it's not real.''

His hands landed on her shoulders, and she found herself spun around and in his arms.

''The hell it's not real,'' he said flatly. ''All that bastard needed to know was that I was sleeping with you. He's been following me anyway, because he knew that was the quickest way to find you. The engagement isn't for Linden, it's for me.''

The next day passed without event, except for the changeable weather. One moment it would be pouring with rain, the next the sun was burning down, the intense, humid heat enervating. Roma stayed inside most of the day, which sawed at her nerves. The hut was cramped and dark and hot, and she hadn't thought to bring any reading material with her. Aside from cooking meals and washing the dishes afterward, there was nothing to do.

Ben went out periodically to check his surveillance equipment. Other than that, he spent his time maintaining regular radio checks with each of the members of the team, and noting their positions on a map—a safety procedure to make sure no one got lost or hurt in the rough terrain.

Ben's frustration level built through the day. The weather was hot and steamy, and Roma was lying around in a skimpy halter top and a brief pair of shorts. Every time she shifted restlessly on the bed or flopped on her back, he had to forcibly restrain himself from joining her. With God only knew how many pairs of binoculars trained on the house, he couldn't do a thing about his frustration level but wait until nightfall.

As soon as it got dark, he coaxed her to bed, determined to banish the distance that seemed to be growing between them despite their physical intimacy.

Rain pounded on the windows, seemed to float in the air as they made love. When it was over, they lay tangled together, sweat sealing their skin where they touched. Gradually Roma relaxed beside him, the tension that had kept her restless and on edge during the daylight hours seeping away as she drifted into sleep.

Still too tense to sleep, Ben propped himself on one elbow and watched her as she slept.

They'd made love, and he knew that she loved him, but other than that, she was eluding him. He had no sense that she was his, and it was driving him crazy.

It was as if she'd retreated behind a blank mask, and wherever it was that she'd gone, he couldn't reach her. She hadn't put the engagement ring back on, hadn't said she would marry him, though he wanted to marry *her*. All his uncertainties had dissolved when she'd walked out on him and he'd thought he'd lost her to Linden. But the situation with Linden had had the opposite effect on Roma. The closing out was subtle, but it was there, and it was driving him crazy, because he wanted everything from her. He needed commitment.

He understood the fear that was freezing her up inside, but he wouldn't allow her to use that as a reason for walking away from him. Once Linden was out of the way, things would settle down. He would have time to convince her.

He wrapped his arm around her waist and settled her in close against him, uncaring that it was too hot to cuddle.

Oh yeah, he had time with Roma, he thought grimly...providing he could keep her with him.

At dawn of the third day Ben packed the rucksack with reconstituted food, bottles of water and batteries. He was going to meet West to replenish their supplies.

Roma pulled on her oversize shirt, letting it hang loose over her shorts. "I'm coming with you. I can't stand being cooped up in here another day."

"You should stay out of sight."

"Of what?" she muttered. "The birds?"

Ben looked up from the pack. "I don't want to take any risks with you."

"You keep forgetting one thing," she said calmly, rummaging for her sneakers. "I'm not the target, McCabe. You are."

While Ben was checking the Glock, she slipped the Sig out of her holdall and eased it into the small of her back, then sat on the edge of the bed and laced on her sneakers.

West materialised out of the shadows. He was dressed in army fatigues, the DPM—disruptive pattern material—blending perfectly with the shades of the bush. He took the rucksack and handed over an empty one, then stood talking to Ben.

Roma wandered away, enjoying the soft, cool air of early morning, the pretty wildflowers that sprouted among the rough, tussocky grass. She went down on her knees and began picking a few of the tough little blossoms to brighten up the grim interior of the hut. She snapped a stem of ladder fern then another, adding them to the bunch, then froze. A familiar tension tightened the skin at the centre of her spine, crawled all the way to her nape. The flowers dropped from her grasp. She straightened, turned casually, gaze drifting along the rim of heavy forest.

He was standing, rifle fitted to his shoulder, scope to his eye, bringing the gun to bear on Ben and West. She wouldn't have seen him at all if he hadn't moved in the precise moment her gaze passed over him, because, like West, he was wearing army fatigues and blended so perfectly with the bush around him that he was all but invisible.

She didn't yell, afraid that he would shoot if he heard her. She simply pulled out the Sig, thumbing the safety off as she swung the gun up, levelled and fired, and kept firing systematically. There was a moment of startled eye contact, then the man ducked out of sight.

"Damn it all to hell," Ben roared. "Get *down*."

A heavy weight crashed into her side, the gun was knocked from her hands, and Ben's arms wrapped around her as she fell sideways, cushioning her as they hit the ground. The whine of a bullet stung in her ears, followed by a hollow report that echoed across the hills. A second shot followed; dirt and grass exploded a bare foot away.

West's voice came deep and cool and unshakeable from the edge of the bush. "Move. *Now*."

She caught the blur of shadows as West stepped from the cover of the trees, the Ruger fitted to his shoulder, swinging in a smooth arc.

Ben's arms clamped tighter around her, his body

shielding her as they rolled, sky whirling past in a kaleidoscope of brilliant blue and fluffy white clouds. Something hard jolted her shoulder, the root of a tree; then she was half dragged behind a thick gnarled trunk.

West's heart pumped hard as he caught the shiver of leaves, the glint of sun on metal, and was startled by the ice-pure magnification of a tanned face, a shock of dark blond hair. Deliberately, he adjusted his aim lower and let the breath sift from between his teeth.

The Ruger kicked back into his shoulder. The echo kept going, ricocheting off granite faces, finally absorbed by the dense hush of the bush. He sighted the scope again for confirmation, keeping Linden's collapsed figure in his crosshairs.

He was aware of Ben and Roma lying on the ground a few metres away. "You can get up now. He's down."

Ben ignored West, who was already walking toward Linden, with Carter covering him. He was too intent on the woman lying half beneath him in the damp grass. His heart had nearly stopped when he'd turned to see her shooting at Linden as calmly as if she were on a shooting range. She could have died. He framed her face, his hands shaking. "Don't ever do that to me again."

Roma reached up and brushed a smudge of dirt from his jaw. "I'll do it as many times as I like. He was trying to kill you."

Ben went still inside, all the hairs at the back of his nape lifting. He began to understand just what kind of woman he'd got. "If you'll risk your life for me, then you'll damn well marry me without any more argument, because I don't want to live without you."

A tear trickled down her cheek. She blinked and sniffed. "Is that a proposal or an order, McCabe?"

He framed her face with his hands, his thumbs brushing at the tears. "Yeah, I know, I'm so romantic," he said softly. "You bet it's a proposal, and I'm not taking 'No' for an answer."

"Bingo," West said coldly. "Our hit man."

Carter terminated radio contact, pushed his lip mike out of the way and nudged Linden with his booted foot. The man moaned with pain and clutched his leg. Carter saw with savage satisfaction that Linden also had blood streaming down one arm from a deep gash on his bicep. West had only used one shot, so that piece of damage belonged to Roma. She hadn't managed to stop Linden, but she'd winged him, numbing his right arm and spoiling his aim. But the fact that West had only used one bullet and Linden had two wounds posed a problem. The police liked closure in these matters, and a mystery gunman would keep them awake nights.

"West," Carter said briefly, "we've got two wounds here. Why don't you shoot your gun again so the equation works?"

West aimed the Ruger skyward and discharged a second shot, then calmly reloaded and trained the gun on Linden.

Carter ignored Linden's moans while he searched for weapons; he had his priorities, and Linden's health and well-being ranked somewhere around the zero mark—way below putting out the trash and deciding whether or not to take a trip to the laundrette.

"He's clean," he said curtly. He opened a pouch on his belt, pulled out a pair of thin latex gloves and pulled them on. "I'm going to give you a shot of morphine," he said to the man on the ground. "Then I'll bandage you while we wait for the chopper. Do you understand me?"

The man rasped agreement, but Carter still had to prise his hands loose from his bleeding thigh and repeat his words several times before he got Linden's trouser leg cut away from the wound.

"You're lucky," he continued flatly. "Neither bullet severed an artery, so you won't bleed out. You're in a lot of pain, because muscle tissue's torn and the muscles around the injuries are contracting, making the pain worse, but it's nothing you can't handle. You'll be fit to stand trial."

He broke open the small combat syrette of morphine and stabbed it into a knotted thigh muscle. Seconds later Linden relaxed with a groan, and Carter pulled out a couple of tampons. "I've always wanted to do this," he murmured as he inserted dense tubes of cotton into both the entrance and exit wounds.

"Should help you get in touch with your feminine side."

The tampons immediately soaked up blood and swelled, stemming the steady seepage. He applied pads and bandaging, then moved on to the arm wound.

A four-wheel drive came to a halt just metres away. Blade climbed out. "The chopper's five minutes away, the police team will be here in two." He stared down at Linden. He looked younger than the fifty-two years his passport claimed, and he was tanned and fit, something they hadn't expected when they'd found out he was dying of cancer. All the medical evidence had suggested he shouldn't be capable of the feat of endurance he'd just carried out. He'd had a rough sea landing, then he'd had to scale cliffs in the dark and walk several miles in dense rain forest, the going treacherously slippery with all the rain they'd had. The trek in should have killed him.

He shook his head. "He must have reconnoitred, then come in from the coast last night. One of the team just spotted a small runabout, pulled up on the beach."

The distant beat of rotor blades sounded on the air. Blade checked his watch, then switched his attention to West, who had slung the Ruger over his shoulder and was leaning against a tree, watching Linden. "Nice shot," he commented. "You kept him alive."

West's mouth curled slightly at one corner. "I aim to please. Your sister gave me some leeway. She punched the first hole in him. He had trouble aiming after that."

Blade's expression sharpened. "Roma's armed?"

West's half smile turned into a lazy grin. "It wasn't McCabe's gun this time. She was carrying her own weapon." He eyed Linden's arm. "Nice shooting, for a handgun. That girl's got talent."

Blade swore softly, appalled. "She brought her gun with her." His eyes closed. *She had actually brought her gun with her.* The gun *he* had given her because she'd pestered him so often to let her shoot his.

The ramifications began to pile up.

She'd carried the gun illegally out of one country and into another. God only knew how she'd managed to weasel it through customs. Then she'd shot a man who was on Interpol's Most Wanted list with it. She hadn't left a bullet in him as evidence, which was something. "Did anyone actually see her shoot Linden?"

Carter straightened from strapping Linden's arm, peeled his gloves off and zipped them into a disposable plastic bag. "I don't know about anyone else," he said mildly, "but I didn't see your sister shoot anyone. I was too busy covering West's sorry ass. He had to shoot twice. Must be losing his touch."

Linden's eyes flickered open, slightly dreamy, and

fastened on West. "Why didn't you go for the head shot?"

West eyed the man who had executed Jake Lombard, stalked Roma, and tried to kill Ben. All people he cared for. He was thirty years old, and in all those years he could count the people he cared for and still not reach double digits. There was a hot rage in him when he looked at Linden, and coldness. He knew what Linden was asking. He'd stood still for that shot. West hadn't obliged him.

Gray and Blade needed to talk to Linden. The whole Lombard family needed closure for Jake. West would be damned if he would deprive them of that just because Linden wanted a mercy killing. If his medical condition was correct, he would die soon enough, anyway, but with a bit of luck, he would get his day in court first.

He met Linden's gaze, studied the stoic acceptance he saw there, and answered the question.

"Too much paperwork," he replied softly.

Epilogue

Linden didn't make it to trial, but he confessed before he finally passed away in a prison hospital, providing details of his illegal activities over the years, including the approximate location at sea where he'd carried out the execution of Rafaella and Jake.

The Lombard family held a small ceremony as close as possible to the spot where they thought Jake had been lost. He was gone, but at least they had a measure of peace, and the knowledge that the threat that had dominated their lives for so many years, first from Harper and then from Linden, was finally gone. And the sense of lightness at finally being free of the events that had started with Jake's death was amplified by the anticipation of a wedding looming on the horizon.

* * *

The wedding was small, and was held in Bridget and Guido Lombard's garden. It didn't make any social pages, because the Lombards knew how to do things quietly when they wanted. The ceremony was strictly family and close friends, which made it a bun fight in anyone's terminology.

The bride wore white, the dress filched straight off the catwalk of Evan diVaggio's scene-stealing collection. The groom was handsome in his morning suit, with no Kevlar body armour or weaponry in sight. The groom had also made it his business to search the bride before the ceremony, and the hell with tradition. He hadn't put it past her to stash a gun somewhere. When he'd lifted her skirt, to the outrage of Bridget Lombard—who was despairing of getting her daughter to the altar with any semblance of propriety—he hadn't found a gun, he'd found something far more dangerous: the garter belt.

The sight of that lacy little confection wrapped around his wife-to-be's sleek thigh still had the power to make him break out in a sweat.

The ceremony was simple and moving; however, when it came to signing the register, tradition went out the window. McCabe's new wife refused to sign unless she had her list of demands met. McCabe read the list, which resembled nothing so much as a hard-ass ransom note.

His beloved wanted flowers and romantic candle-lit dinners, and breakfast in bed every Sunday—he got his turn on Saturday. She wanted jewelry and perfume and lingerie—nothing nylon in the lingerie department or the deal was off. And if he ever waved a condom at her again, she would probably shoot him.

The demands were feminine and outrageous.

McCabe sighed.

Carter was the best man, and one of Roma's long-standing girlfriends from boarding school was brides-maid. The flower girl, the only kid with McCabe after her name at the wedding, fidgeted in her matching white gown and coronet of fresh flowers, and prac-tised batting her lashes at the handsome, tanned, Lombard cousin who was page-boy. He was eight years old and fascinating, and she decided she might just marry him. If he behaved himself.

He didn't. Things got a little rocky when Bunny got into a food fight with her escort. After dispatch-ing him with a slug to the eye, she announced in a penetrating voice that she may be the only McCabe kid now, but that was about to change. Her dad had told her that pretty soon there were going to be a whole lot more McCabes, so he'd better watch it.

The bride resolved the small silence that rippled through the gathering by briskly tossing her bouquet in the general direction of her school friend, who was too bedazzled by the attentions of the best man to notice.

The fragrant, delicate bouquet of white roses ended up in the lean, battle-scarred hands of Gabriel West.

McCabe decided that the garter was absolutely not being thrown. Like the bride, the garter belonged to him.

* * * * *

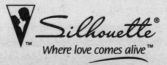